Patricia Schonstein grew up in Zimbabwe and now lives in South Africa. Her first novel was the award-winning *Skyline*. She has a master's degree in creative writing from the University of Cape Town.

THE APOTHECARY'S DAUGHTER

A nobleman and his wife, an apothecary nun, an astronomer-mathematician, an inquisitor, a poet, a portraitist, a queen and loyal servants act out a drama of tantalizing relationships. They take up their roles in castle and convent; some are surrounded by ornate interiors, garbed in velvets and silks, while others abide in simple space, dressed in plain linens and dull calicos . . . This is a wondrous tale, rendered in beautiful and erotic prose and poetry. A story of inquisition, book burning, persecution and intolerance of new knowledge, it also depicts trade and exotic travel, both across the earth and among the stars.

PATRICIA SCHONSTEIN

THE APOTHECARY'S DAUGHTER

Complete and Unabridged

ULVERSCROFT
Leicester

First published in Great Britain in 2004 by
Bantam Press
a division of
Transworld Publishers
London

First Large Print Edition
published 2005
by arrangement with
Transworld Publishers
a division of
The Random House Group Ltd
London

British Library CIP Data

Schonstein, Patricia
    The apothecary's daughter.—Large print ed.—
    Ulverscroft large print series: historical fiction
    1. Africa—North—History—*1517 – 1882*—Fiction
    2. Historical fiction 3. Large type books
    I. Title
    823.9′14 [F]

    ISBN 1–84617–024–9

Published by
F. A. Thorpe (Publishing)
Anstey, Leicestershire

Set by Words & Graphics Ltd.
Anstey, Leicestershire
Printed and bound in Great Britain by
T. J. International Ltd., Padstow, Cornwall

This book is printed on acid-free paper

For Don and Emmanuel —
travellers both

Acknowledgements

It has been a delight to work with my agent, Stephanie Cabot, and my editor, Francesca Liversidge, in the production of this novel. I thank them for their enthusiasm in my work, and for their invaluable contribution.

All the world's a stage, and all the men and women merely players ...

William Shakespeare

I render infinite thanks to God, for being so kind as to make me alone the first observer of marvels kept hidden in obscurity for all previous centuries.

Galileo Galilei

The Main Players
The Nobleman
The Noblewoman
The Apothecary Nun
The Astronomer-Mathematician
The Jeweller
The Queen
The Inquisitor
The Serving Woman
The Travelling Actors

The Minor Players
The Holy Sisters
The Riders
The Red Miners
The Portraitist
The Travelling Surgeon
The Convent Gardener
The Convent Priest
The Monk
The Astronomer-Mathematician's
Serving Boy
The Astronomer-Mathematician's
Italian Friend
The Tavern Keeper
The Violator

Various Nubian Free Slaves and Servants of
the Castle including the Keeper of Bees
Various Merchants and Traders in Fine
Artefacts
Various Tavern Patrons

The Setting

Somewhere in North Africa, not far inland
from the Mediterranean, where Phoenicians,
Romans and Greeks once left their mark
and where the doctrine of the Holy Roman
Church now rules

Part One

I looked for your bones;
there were so many strewn across the
outskirts of the town
that all I could do was line them up:
tibiae fibulae finger-bones skulls teeth
splinters.
I placed them neatly, and for each bone
wrote a poem,
hoping that at least one was yours.
How is it that everything recurs?
That no lesson is learnt from war or
genocide?
The story of hell can be told in every
country, in every time:
The book-burning, the inquisition, the
ghetto, the death by fire belong to us all.
How sad I am for this.

The Bone Gatherer

Leonardo Capelutto, the nobleman, fetched his betrothed on a winter's day from the convent where she was born, when she was nineteen years old. Until then the only men she had ever known were the aged gardener who worked for the nuns, and the even older myopic priest who came each Sunday to offer Mass.

She knew nothing of the world. The nuns had kept her hair cut short, so it hung straight and thick at shoulder length, and dressed her in simple beige calico shifts. She had been taught to sew, spin and weave coarse cotton and wool; to extract the essential medicinal properties of herbs and barks and flowers; but had never felt the texture of silk or damask or seen garments made of fabrics dyed to rich colours. She had never read manuscripts or books that were not religious, so had no understanding of the known world. Because the doors and shutters of the convent were closed each evening at sunset, she had never properly looked at the stars and planets or watched their positioning and movement in the night sky. A life lived without the order

3

and regulation of prayer was unknown to her.

The nobleman came for her on horseback, accompanied by his men, who emerged from the morning mist, riding down the stony road that led to the convent, the brass and iron of their saddlery jangling, their huge black stallions snorting hot breath into the cold air.

She was ready and waiting for him. The nuns, fussed and anxious, had helped her to prepare, drawing water from the well, standing round her as she washed in the pre-dawn, candlelit dark of their communal bathing cell; watching her rub herself dry with a coarse towel; warming skin which cringed against the cold water. They hovered while she dressed, and sat with her before the breakfast they had set in the dining room — porridge with soured milk and a square of wild honeycomb, a rarity which the gardener, saddened by her imminent departure, had procured; he too had known her as a baby and watched her grow into a fine young woman. But she was anxious and her stomach was knotted, so she could not eat.

She sat at the portal with a basket at her side packed for the journey — a change of garment; a loaf of rye bread and a quarter-round of cheese; olives and a flagon of the first pressed oil; a bar of lye soap; the square of gold honeycomb in a lidded clay pot; a bunch of dried rosemary, the herb of remembrance.

Only the apothecary, her mother, the nun who had been closest to her, who had cared for her as a child then taught her the constituents of plants and herbs, came out of the convent walls to speak briefly with the nobleman. It seemed to the girl that they knew each other well, that they were more than just business acquaintances, for though they did not appear to touch one another there was a warmth between them, as there might be between deep friends who had not seen each other for many years.

The other nuns stayed within the walls, did not come out to bid farewell, only squeezed her hand, then nudged her, pushed her away from the world inside into the perilous world beyond. They watched the girl through the grille, each taking a turn to glimpse her departure and bless her as she went. The apothecary pressed a small wooden cross into her daughter's palm, then held her close and kissed her before turning away hurriedly so the moment of parting was not prolonged.

'Theodora, you must live each day of your life as though it be your last,' the apothecary had said on the eve of her departure. 'Cherish it as a jewel; harm nothing and no one. Go about your life as though in prayer, as though each day be a prayer bead on a rosary; as though your whole life be a thread of beaded homage.'

The nobleman threw a cloak of finely woven wool about the girl; pulled the hood, trimmed with black astrakhan, over her head, closed it at her neck with a cameo of onyx, seemed not to notice the wetness of her eyes, said nothing. He gave her a pair of kidskin gloves, waiting as she pulled them on, then helped her mount, guiding a sandalled foot into each stirrup, spreading the cloth of her shift to allow her legs to part across the saddle, tucking the folds of the cloak under it. He placed the reins in her hands then mounted his own horse, which whinnied as he led his men and the girl, in a line, with her third from the end, up through the mist and out of the valley. This was to be her first journey and she noticed, as they set off and she saw the convent from the outside for the first time, that poppies grew there, as they did within the convent, and that they were in deep sanguine bloom, whereas those within were still in bud.

Behind her, the nuns prepared themselves for a life without her, and the convent walls sighed with their lamentations. Before her, the world began to unfold.

They travelled north-east and her skin, which had never before felt roughness, became red and sore from the rubbing of the saddle and the flanks of the horse. Her back ached. Because she had only experienced the enclosed and ordered reality within the convent walls, this outside world, filled with a cacophony of bird and insect sound, seemed to stretch on and on arbitrarily, without obvious pattern. It changed in texture and scale, washing through her until she felt light-headed. She held tight to her horse, fearing she might fall and be consumed by the vastness about her; feeling as though she stood on the edge of an abyss, knowing nothing of what lay before her; having to wait for life to unfurl. At the cardinal points of the day and night, she knew which prayers the holy sisters would be reciting, and imagined them in the dark chapel with its single candle burning, the smell of wax permeating the air.

Leonardo Capelutto and his riders were clothed in coarse cotton shirts, leather trousers, doublets and cloaks, and spurred boots which reached their knees. Each had a scabbard and sword on his left side, a dagger on his right and a small bow and quiver of arrows on his back. Their faces were browned and creviced by sun and their hair was long (the nobleman's held in a single thick plait and the riders' either tied back or left loose and knotted and wild). Across their broad horses each carried a blanket roll and a leather bag, and she (who had few possessions of her own) wondered what they kept inside.

Theodora had never known the company of so many men — men who were so rough, so wild in appearance, so deep in voice and blunt in manner, so very opposite to the women she had shared her life with. They smelt pungent, like wild grass, and sour, like fermented sap.

The nobleman brought her water in a leather bowl at the start and end of each day so she could bathe her face and hands. She noted, glancing furtively so as not to seem to stare, that he was tall and strongly built, that his thick black plait reached down his back to his waist, that his hands were long and slender, though rough and scarred by weather and time, like his face; that he had no beard.

They camped in the night openness; she in a tent of muslin, he and his men on sleeping mats, wrapped in their cloaks, under the stars. They cooked over open fires — grain which they boiled into a porridge; hare or bird which one of them had shot; wild herbs which grew along the way; wine which was not as sweet as the convent wine; the bread, olives and cheese which the nuns had procured. He brought food to her on a pewter plate with wine in a pewter cup. She ate alone, apart from the men, beside the tent on a carpet that had been spread for her. She had never before been left alone, away from a group; had never eaten outdoors or partaken of a meal that was not blessed. In the deep darkness after the moon had set and before the sun rose, she would hold the small cross. The apothecary had carved it from rosewood; it was still rough, had not been smoothed through hours of meditation.

The nobleman said little to her, asked now and then after her comfort, spoke only to his men around the fire, while she lay on her rug under muslin beneath a star-filled sky, attentive to the hugeness of the earth and the darkness of the outside night. His voice was lighter than those of his men, which were coarse and deep, and she listened to it amongst theirs, and to the sounds of the night which had no convent walls to contain them, but which spread on and on to the edge of the earth. In the far distance wolves howled; flocks of night-birds flew overhead in a whoosh of wing movement.

★   ★   ★

After five days they reached the nobleman's home. They arrived at night, and only the next morning would Theodora see that it was a small castle with creeper-covered, crenellated walls on the edge of an escarpment overlooking a river and a town.

Nubian servants wearing long robes and carrying burning braziers came out to meet them, greeting them warmly. The nobleman helped the girl from her horse, steadying her as she stumbled in weariness, taking her cloak from her shoulders and handing it to one of the Nubians, an elderly, slightly hunched woman. The woman greeted her, taking the gloves from the girl's hands and saying simply, 'I am Halla, and I welcome you with my whole heart.'

Urged by the nobleman, Theodora followed Halla through the main carved wooden door into a hallway, illuminated by candles and oil lamps that threw light against high stained-glass windows. In the very far distance, the sea washed the shore, and the wind bore from it the smell of salt and shells. 'Go with Halla,' he said. 'She will show you your room, and help you refresh yourself. You must rest for a few days, after our long journey.'

Halla led her up a stone staircase, lined with tall, gilt-framed, dark portraits of men and women in high lace collars; and across a landing peopled with white marble statues; then into a large room with a curtained bed in the centre, two carved wooden chests, a stone table, and large windows open to a dramatic moonlit view across the land. The marble floor was spread with Persian carpets, elaborately patterned in dull gold and madder.

Here Halla undid the ties of the girl's shift, undressed her and led her behind a screen where stood a granite tub of warm scented water. Into this the girl stepped and the servant washed her gently with white savon, wetting her short hair, lathering it, soaping her whole body then rinsing her with a jug, drying her, laying her on the stone table and oiling her with sweet fragrances that rose into the air. The servant rubbed cooling cream on to the roughened and red skin of the girl's inner thighs, and her hands. The soothing perfumes caused her eyes to fill with tears, but she did not cry.

The woman then dressed her in a sleeping robe of embossed silk and showed her to the bed, where she lay between sheets of finely woven linen embroidered in blackwork. 'Don't leave me,' whispered the girl. 'I have never been alone.'

'I will watch over you, but you have nothing to fear,' answered Halla.

The girl slept deeply and dreamt of nothing save the sounds of metal harnesses and the hooves of horses against rock and the calls of wild birds interlaced with sung prayer.

When she awoke, Halla was sitting waiting for her, sewing. On a table at the side of the bed, covered by a square of cloth, were bread, cheese, olives, melon preserve, ripe figs, grape juice and a small carafe of olive oil. 'Eat, child,' the woman urged, rising and uncovering the food, then drawing open the curtains of the high window nearest the bed, so the view across the escarpment, with the town nestled beside the river, stood before them like a painting in which only birds moved.

In the convent, the apothecary sat at her workbench, numbed by loss, unable to do anything but stare at sage and sweet basil spread before her, dried and ready to be crushed and stored away.

★ ★ ★

Some days later Theodora asked after the nobleman, for she had not seen him since he brought her here, to his castle. He had left, Halla told her, early on the morning after their arrival and would be away some weeks.

Leonardo Capelutto was a traveller and cartographer. He was often away. She was simply to wait for him. She could come and go as she pleased: could wander through the walled garden where grew only plants which flowered in white, through the vineyards, through the farmlands where gold barley and wheat waved in the sunlight, and through the vegetable plots where pumpkins and marrow wound their determined way into the twisted branches of crabapple and pear trees.

The nobleman had left instructions for the woman-servant to attend her every need. The girl was to want for nothing. Only, she was not to leave the estate or go to the Nubians' cottages, nor down to the town.

Theodora sat on her balcony, twisting at the stuff of her dress, picking at its decorative beads, flooded with emotions of homesickness and abandonment. The northerly wind carried the smell of the sea. With a sense that perhaps she had made a mistake in coming, she suddenly wanted to return to the convent, to the women she knew, to the apothecary's room with its familiar fragrances of ointments and tinctures and dried plants, to her small cell, to the reassuring sounds of prayer and devotions and striking bells, to the simple emptiness, to the absence of colour. But this vast, many-roomed palace, filled with the sumptuous richness of textiles and carved works, was now her home. The nobleman, the apothecary had told her, was a benefactor of the convent. He had tithed an annual sum to the holy order for many years and, in addition, had paid a handsome bride-price to the cloistered women for the girl. She could not go back. She was no longer a child. To return would mean to take on religious vows and become a nun. This had all been explained to her, and she had agreed to become a bride in the world rather than a bride of God. But nothing had prepared her for the splendour that enclosed her, nor the aloneness.

She asked her woman-servant for the basket the nuns had given her, and the dress she had arrived in, and the second one; and what was left of the rye bread, the olives, her flagon of oil; the honeycomb. She wanted her sandals. 'Halla, what have you done with my soap? And there was my small washing flannel with it. You must give me my belongings back,' she said. 'I want the pouch of dried herbs that was with my things.'

'Did you not eat the bread and cheese, and the olives, child? On the journey here?' asked her servant with concern. 'I found no honeycomb when I unpacked for you. Nor the dried herbs you speak of, for that matter.

But I'll bring you honey, if you want some. The master keeps his own hives. His bees feed on wild flowers and in his orchards. There is no honey sweeter than theirs. And if you want herbs, we have a herb garden, just beyond the kitchen. I'll take you down to the gardener later, and you will see what he grows — borage, verbena, lavender, mustard and others.

'I'll look for your basket in the scullery. As for your dresses, well, the master does not want you to wear the cotton of the convent and common folk. I have made your new garments. Months before you arrived they were sewn and ready for you. Look. Here they are, all folded in the chests. You have only to choose which to wear. You can change as often in the day as you wish. And when you see me sewing and embroidering, know it is for you that I work. Do you not like the kidskin shoes on your feet? Are they not comfortable? The soap, it was coarse soap, was it not? Here you will have fine soap, fragranced and soft. Oil, you'll always find at your bedside. There is everything you need here. You have only to ask me. I am here to serve you.

'Do you want me to oil your skin now?' she asked kindly. 'Come, child, let me rub some into you, it will make you feel better. And let

15

me lay a cooling poultice on your brow. Shall I fetch something from the kitchen for you? Perhaps you are hungry. Would you like some bread with conserve, or slices of meat?'

Theodora shook her head, and stayed sitting on the balcony, the small rosewood cross held tight in her hand. When night fell the music of reed flutes, drums and tambourines drifted up from the Nubians' cottages on the edge of the estate. The old woman slept in a chair next to the girl, so she would not feel alone, and the next morning brought her the convent basket with the calico dresses folded in it, her sandals and other belongings, which the cook had stored away in the kitchen.

★ ★ ★

On the first night that the nobleman was back, he and Theodora ate together in the dining hall, at a large oak table laden with food and flowers. Halla did not stand waiting, but came in only when he struck the small gong at the side of his place setting.

Theodora was filled with excitement and expectation. Halla had bathed and oiled her and dressed her in a shift of carmine linen, embroidered down the front and fastened with small jasper buttons. She had massaged her feet and given her new moleskin shoes to wear, and an ankle bracelet of silver. Round her neck Halla hung a single strand of cabochon sapphires.

Candelabra lit the dining hall. The brass fittings and table crystal gleamed in the flickering candlelight. In the corners of the room stood bronze urns filled with freshly picked lilies.

Leonardo wore a white blouson with full, pleated sleeves embroidered in gold thread, a black damask bolero, black pantaloons and embossed leather boots, buckled at the ankles, which reached to his knees. He brought his plait of thick hair round so it draped on his shoulder as he leant heavily on the table, looking across at her, smiling. Now, observing him properly for the first time, she noted that there was a dark beauty about him and that fine features belied the strong masculinity she had seen in him on the ride here. He smelt of sandalwood.

They dined on honeyed duck and stewed venison, pilaff, cheese and bread; crystallized fruits; squares of date cake. She ate heartily and asked for more of everything and he laughed at her, for he knew that in the convent she had eaten plain and repetitious meals of porridge and spinach and coarse breads.

Leonardo poured wine for each of them and lifted his gold-rimmed goblet to her happiness, watched by the still, timeless portraits that hung against the walls. The wine was stronger than she was accustomed to, and it rushed to her head in a wash of lightness.

'I drink to you, Theodora, my young betrothed,' he said, looking at her with deep, sincere eyes. 'And I welcome you to your home. Here you are mistress and your every desire will be granted. You shall want for nothing, my dear.'

With the wine playing against her composure and tinselling her responses, she was too shy to say anything, and merely smiled at him, thinking, I am the betrothed of a nobleman. I am the only one of us to be betrothed. She glanced up at the paintings above the fireplace.

The nobleman struck the gong, and called for the candles and lamps to be lit upstairs.

It was on this night that he first made love to her.

★ ★ ★

Leonardo Capelutto led Theodora up to her room and began with the undoing of the small jasper buttons down the back of her dress. He untied the knots of her vest, and took her garments off, dropping them to the floor. Then he showed her to the bed, where she sat, unclothed, trembling and apprehensive, as he tied back the curtains, for she knew nothing of men save what little the apothecary had explained. She watched him undo his plait and pull his long black hair forward so that it fell heavily, parted in the centre and reaching down to his waist, and was startled by his dark beauty.

He ran his hands across her shoulders, down her arms, touched her breasts, lingered there. She stared down at her feet, unable to look at him. He put a thumb under her chin and lifted her face, gently; circled his palm about the smoothness of her neck; seemed not to notice the wetness in her eyes.

The skin of his hands was rough against her softness. He unclasped the sapphire necklace, knelt down and took the moleskin shoes from her feet, undid the anklet. Then he blew out each candle, and pinched the wicks of the oil lamps so their light was extinguished. In the dark he came to her, fully clothed.

All Leonardo did that first night was kiss her. He kissed her lips and her neck, her stomach. He kissed her feet above and on the soles; ran his hands up her legs, working her

19

flesh as though it were clay, river clay from which fine bowls are fashioned. When she reached up to hold him, he took her arms and pinned them down. He would not let her touch him. He alone touched and felt and gave pleasure on that first night, his long hair falling all about her like silk, the finely woven linen of his garments caressing her so she burst into flame, panting like a small forest animal, aroused towards something primal, wanting something she had never known before. But he did not enter her. He merely tantalized her and then quietened her with his hands and his lips and his tongue. When he was done, and she lay spent with pleasure, he closed the fine curtains around her bed, and left her to go and sleep in his own quarters.

Theodora lay in the darkness, naked under the bedcover, aware of Halla coming in when he went out. The woman lit a single candle, picked up the clothes and shoes and jewellery from the floor, tidied them away then sat at the window, dozing on and off until daybreak.

The next day he was gone. He would be away a month, fetching a consignment of goods which he had stored across the sea, at the port city of Cadiz. He left a small perfume bottle for her, carved of alabaster and filled with Persian oil, the essence of carnation, and instructed Halla to serve her crystallized fruit each morning that he was away.

★ ★ ★

In this time Theodora wandered about the castle, at first with Halla always behind, stooped and silent in her felt slippers which made no sound against the marbled and carpeted floors, until she asked to be left alone. She walked along the turret, sat there looking out over the fields and at the Nubians who tended them, their blue-black colour contrasted against the gold of the wheat. While they worked they wore only loincloths, and their skin shone with wet sweat. She looked out across the vineyards and olive groves; at the town, below and beyond, and at the line of the sea on the far, far horizon. She explored each room, calling Halla to draw back the heavy velvet curtains from the great lead-paned windows so that light poured in and gave life to the marble statues, the paintings and the silverware and gilded mirrors which enriched the interiors. She marvelled at the exotic and ingenious geometrical patterns of the mosaic floors in some of the rooms, and the painted ceilings; stood in awe under the dome of the entrance hall, decorated in blue and gold and revealing the genius of a Byzantine artist; she ran her hands across the masterfully worked tapestries and the rich carpets.

In the convent, the halls and rooms were bare save for a simple wooden crucifix nailed in each room and a statue of the Virgin Mary, carved from grey granite and uncoloured, which stood in the chapel; no paintings hung from the walls; no frescoes offered an escape into the mysterious workings of art; the floors were uncovered and the small windows, high up on the walls, delivered no outside view. The stone stairs were worn by centuries of women's sandalled feet. Here in the castle, the marble steps had withstood the wear of the walk of nobility.

Apart from the sounds which came in through the windows — calls of birds, shrilling of insects, the noises of the working farmlands, the songs in the evenings from the Nubians' cottages — all was quiet. And no one spoke to her, unless she spoke first, for she was mistress of the estate and all others here were her servants.

No visitors came while the nobleman was away, though emissaries delivered sealed letters that were placed on his desk, awaiting his return. He was clearly a man who conducted much correspondence. When she asked Halla about him — who he was, who his family were — the woman told her that he was a man of high birth; that he was blood-linked to various aristocratic families; that the Queen's confessor was his cousin; that his mother had died in childbirth bearing him and a twin; and that his father had departed this life, an old broken-hearted man, when the twin met a tragic death in the desert regions.

But all this Theodora already knew, for the apothecary had told her. She had hoped Halla would tell her more. She asked about the black men who tilled the fields and took care of the livestock and bees. 'They were once slaves here, as I was,' explained the old lady, 'captured and sold to my master's father by Moorish traders. My master freed us when his father died. We are free to go. But we know no other home. And our backs are branded with the mark of bondage. We would simply be captured again and sold to one harsher than our master.'

Theodora looked closely at Halla's face and the lines which coursed around her eyes, wondering what life she had once been taken from. She turned to look out of her window at the bent backs of the black men as they worked. She found her mind chorusing the adorations and hymns of the holy sisters. She missed the chanting and bells of the convent, longed for the hum of sung prayer and for the smells of simple life — plain bread and broths; lye soap; the dried herbs of the apothecary's room. Living alone while Leonardo travelled, she did not want for conversation, for she had grown up knowing measured speech and long times of silence. But she longed for sisterhood and the companionship of women.

Now, looking at the Nubians, she wondered what they longed for, and turned back to face Halla, but saw only her retreating figure as she left the room, closing the door quietly behind herself.

★ ★ ★

The sounds of their horses heralded the second return of the nobleman and his riders. From the far distance came the clinking of saddlery and the striking of hooves and the weary laments of travelled men. Theodora hurried outside and waited.

When Leonardo rode into view, leading his men through the late-afternoon sunlight, she ran up to his horse and he reined it in as it shied and threw its head up. Dismounting, he bowed to her, greeting her with warmth and tenderness, then took her in his arms, so she smelt his sourness and stale perspiration. His men rode on towards the stables, leading his

24

horse with them, and he strolled with his arm about her to the front door, throwing down his cape, wiping his brow, his spurs striking the step as he wiped mud from his boots.

'Let me bathe now, and try to find myself under all this dirt and dust,' he said, laughing. 'Will you dine and drink with me, once I am clean and recognizable?' They walked upstairs together and he kissed her on the landing.

Leonardo went to his own quarters, where he washed and attired, while Theodora chose to be dressed in a robe of jade woven through with silver filaments, and for her hair to be threaded with small beads.

They met in the dining hall as night darkened and candles illuminated the room, sitting at places set with plates of roast lamb and onions and round millet cakes. Later, when they had finished their meal, he took her hand and led her into a room where his riders had unpacked leather cases of the treasures he had brought back. These were laid out on an oak table and on the carpets that covered the floor.

Theodora gasped at the splendour before her. Intricately worked and patterned silver crosses lined the table. Some were inset with jewels — carnelian, aquamarine, beryl and citrine. Others were simple but solid and heavy. On the carpets were placed statues, torsos of women carved from fragrant wood.

In one of the leather bags was a Bedouin marriage gown, beaded and filigreed. Leonardo gave this to her, and a veil of gold netting. Then he opened a round iron-wood box, patterned with ivory inlay and just larger than the palm of her hand. Inside was a string of amber beads, reds and oranges with insects and leaves trapped within their timeless depths, and two thick wedding bands of white gold. He hung the amber around her neck, asking, 'Will you accept if I choose to marry you at the new moon?'

'I will,' she whispered.

'Then I have another gift for you. Come with me,' he said, laughing as he took her down to the kitchen, taking two steps at a time so she almost stumbled keeping up with him. There, perched in a wicker cage, was a large jungle bird, plumed in scarlet and turquoise. 'I will always try to bring you back a wild bird. I have called a carpenter to come up from the town to build an aviary, one into which you can walk, which I will fill with song for you.'

Theodora crouched before the bird and it stared back at her with sad yellow eyes.

★ ★ ★

The next day, Leonardo led her into his quarters, where the walls were lined, floor to high ceiling, with leather-bound books and rolled parchments; where a large globe of the world spun at the lightest touch; where an ivory-inlaid screen shielded his dressing and bathing area; and where a simple cotton mattress and folded blanket marked the place he slept. A large desk took up the centre of the room and an ottoman stood beneath a draped window.

He had an astrolabe and a cross-staff, a geometric compass, maps and nautical charts, instruments for measuring and weighing gold and precious stones. He led her out on to a balcony and they looked down to a walled garden, heavily blossomed in white flowers and with a fountain in its centre.

'At my convent,' Theodora told him, 'we had a secluded garden of red poppies. Just red. It was where the holy sisters were buried when they died. Nothing marked their places. Only the red poppies upon and around the mounds.'

'I have seen those poppies,' he said. 'How beautiful they are, red against the green grasses which carpet the unnamed graves.'

'Yes! That is exactly their beauty — red

27

against green. And when they die back the seedheads are brown against the green.'

Behind a heavy locked oak door, a spiral staircase led to a viewing room and a second balcony. This was the highest part of the castle.

Leonardo told her she could enter his quarters whenever he was away — he had nothing to hide from her — but that the oak door to the viewing room would remain locked, and she could only climb the stairway behind it with him.

During the following days, goldsmiths and silversmiths and traders in jewels came to buy from the nobleman, and the room downstairs was soon cleared of its treasure.

The nobleman paid his riders in gold coins and they returned to their homes in the town, where they would wait until summoned for his next journey. In this time they cleaned and serviced muskets, sharpened daggers and swords, bought new arrowheads from the fletcher and repaired and waxed saddles and bridles. They groomed and rested their horses and played with their sons and daughters.

They also took pleasure in their womenfolk, satisfying themselves, for their journey was hard and spartan and left them burning with lust.

★ ★ ★

Leonardo Capelutto married Theodora in the chapel of the castle basement, with only Halla present, and the officiating priest, Brother Matteo, who had ridden up on a mule from the abbey beyond the town. He invited no one, though gifts arrived from the Queen and other nobles in the faraway capital, and also from the Mayor and prominent merchants. The nuns from the convent had given a dowry, which he now presented to Theodora — a length of finely woven linen; a rosary of rosewood beads, each carved bead worn and even through long use; a vial of the essential oil of orange blossom, which she knew the apothecary would have extracted. She knew, too, that the rosary was the apothecary's and her eyes filled with tears, for it would have been the nun's valued only possession.

Natural light entered through narrow slits near the ceiling. The altar was heavy with flowers, and large ecclesiastical candles lined the walls, burning brightly. Frankincense glowed in small coal-fired decanters, delivering its rich fragrance.

The nobleman made three marriage vows: to care for Theodora's well-being, to love her, and to be faithful to her. He asked nothing in return.

Each placed a wedding band on the other's finger and listened to the blessing which the monk bestowed as he pronounced them man and wife. The nobleman lifted the veil from his wife's face and kissed her. 'Until death parts us,' he said. 'Whatever I am able to give you, I will, Donna Theodora Capelutto, my wife. Nay, even after death, for good fortune has smiled upon me in bringing you to my life and ending my loneliness.'

'Until death parts us, my husband, Leonardo Capelutto,' she echoed.

He held her at arm's length, admiring her beauty. He ran a finger over her dark eyebrows, then across her lower lip, opening her mouth slightly. Around her neck he fastened a length of rubies which reached to her waist. On to her wrist he clasped a gold bracelet inset with diamonds and blue tanzanite — sent by the Queen. Little chips of glass, embroidered into the cloth of her gown, reflected candlelight. Narrow bands of beads passed over the shoulders and down the bodice. Her hair, which she still wore cut bluntly at shoulder length, as the nuns had kept it, and which her woman-servant had oiled and rinsed in herbs that morning, shone. On her feet she wore slippers of embossed chamois skin.

'Should I not promise you something?' she

asked in a whisper.

'No, I have no need to bind you with promises. I already have everything, now you are my wife.'

All afternoon and into the early evening, Theodora walked about wearing her marriage gown, with her veil tied around her neck, draped down against her back, fingering the rubies her husband had hung about her collar, wishing he had invited all the nuns from the convent, while he sat overlooking his lands, drinking wine. She had no friends with whom to share her joy, and longed for the holy sisters to see her. She wanted to send them sweet cakes and mead. 'Could they really not have come?' she asked, kneeling before him.

'Fifteen habited women riding mules to get here?' Leonardo replied, laughing, running his hands across her flushed cheeks. 'What a spectacle they would have made. Alas, my sweet love, I have told you already, cloistered nuns go nowhere beyond their convent. Even when they die they venture not out, but are buried in their walled grounds — you know this. Think not of them, but enjoy our wedding day.'

'I was very close to one of the sisters, the apothecary,' said Theodora. 'She cared for me and trained me in the use of herbs. She was the mother who bore me, though all the sisters were mothers to me. I long to see her. I don't want her to forget me. I know she would want to see me in my wedding gown.'

The nobleman looked away. 'She will never forget you. I too knew the apothecary nun, once, long ago,' he said. 'But we, both you and I, can have nothing to do with her. It would only torment her.'

'How did you know her?' she asked.

'She helped me, once, with her skill. I was ill with sepsis, dying from injuries similar to those that killed my twin. We were attacked while travelling in the desert. She saved my life. Now hush,' he said, taking a small cake from the table beside him and feeding it to his bride, licking her lips of the cream that had smudged across them and making her laugh. 'Speak no more of her; leave her in our past, and let us go on with our lives. I cannot dwell upon these memories without feeling pain.'

In the dining hall that night, a feast was spread for the two of them: stuffed peacock, small roast veal, toasted quails, wild mushrooms and millet boiled slowly with wine and herbs; a dessert made of elderberry and fig; a blackberry conserve with soured milk; a tart of honeyed pears and apples; candied citron; halva and baklava. Theodora ate and laughed and was full of joy, and he laughed too, encouraging her: 'Eat, my little one; it gives me pleasure to have you in my life and to see you so radiant.' A trio of musicians played on the landing, and the sounds of their mandolin, viola and flute carved trellised sound through the night.

Brother Matteo and Halla ate outside under a wide awning, with the Nubians and the house servants, and the nobleman's riders and their families. Burning braziers and hanging lanterns gave light. They drank mead and cider and ale and feasted well on spit-roasted boar and pheasants, glazed turnips and couscous. The aromas of succulent meats mingled with those of the fire. Their master had lived alone for many years. It was fitting that he now had a wife and it was hoped that there would soon be an heir. Halla kept leaving her place and going into the dining hall to see that her master and his bride were content, and to ask whether they needed anything, until the nobleman shouted: 'Halla, leave us in peace, for the love of God! Stay out there and be festive, we have no need of you in here. Leave us in peace without having to answer constantly to you about our well-being!'

When the trio of musicians were done, the Nubians brought out their own instruments and played first joyous songs, but later, as the night deepened and alcohol burdened their emotions, they sang the sadder, older songs of their forebears and past times; of broken loves and lost lives; of children captured in war, never to return; of youths seized as slaves to serve on galleys, whipped and rowing until they died, or sent to the treacherous cinnabar mines of Almaden, where they would die the most horrible of early deaths. Their songs lamented fine, young women sold as concubines and used until their beauty and bodies were worn down, only to be sold again to hard and harsh labour until premature death released them from bondage.

★ ★ ★

Later that night, in her room, Leonardo Capelutto undressed his bride, dropping her marriage gown to the floor and stepping back to admire her unblemished body. 'You are so perfect, so unspoilt,' he whispered. Even though it was their wedding night, he extinguished the lights of the candles and oil lamps. He drew the curtains so that moonlight did not break the darkness of the room. He took off his doublet — embroidered with silver thread and pearls — and his damask shirt and lay with her, his long black

34

hair loosened and falling like silk all about her, his muscled body pressed against her. I have a husband, she thought, feeling his sleek hair against her nakedness. I am the only one of all of us who is married.

This time Leonardo allowed her to touch his body; but only his upper body. He had not taken off his linen pantaloons. In the dark, she ran her hands tentatively across his strong shoulders. Her fingers traced his face and the hard muscles of his neck, down his torso, pausing at a raised scar which ran across, from armpit to armpit. The scar of precise, delicate stitches crossed his breastline like a raised knotted cord; like a line of prayer beads. Whoever had closed his wound had done so with the care and exactness of an artist.

He lifted her fingers from the scar and kissed them, whispering, 'Never ask me to show this to you. I do not wish you ever to lay eyes upon it. Think of it only as some fine needlework; a restorative seam.'

'Is this the handwork of the apothecary nun? Is this my mother's stitching?' she asked.

'It is your mother's work,' he said, barely audible.

Outside, the Nubians continued to sing, and the tale of a maiden who waited at the edge of her village for her slave lover to return rose up and filled the night stillness, entwined with the lace of a reed flute and peppered with a shivering tambourine.

Leonardo made love to her as he had done on their first night together, and as he would throughout their marriage, half clothed, in the dark, caressing but never penetrating her. He slept beside her that night, close to her so she could smell the wine on his breath, but left her bed before dawn brought any light to them. She turned her face into the pillow, where his head had lain, and breathed in the smell of sandalwood he left behind.

In the convent the nuns lay quiet in their cells, under old, darned blankets, their bodies wrapped in coarse, abrasive sleeping garments that numbed all sensual pleasure, each thinking about the girl who had left their lives and taken with her their fountainhead of joy. They thought about her body and its new role, its movement away from the virginal towards the profane. They were afraid, all of them, for they had allowed their beloved to go forth into a corporeal territory experienced but once (and violently) by only one of them.

★　★　★

36

A portraitist came from the town some weeks later, commissioned by Leonardo to paint his wife. The artist positioned Theodora in the salon against a window, opening the drapes so that he could capture the landscape framed by the window behind her. He set up his easel and opened his box of paints, assessing the light and the shadows in the room, noting the paleness of her skin and determining how best to set this off. He wondered why the wife of so rich a nobleman, one known to the royal house, wore her hair cut bluntly, in so austere a fashion, when she could afford to wear it long and augmented with wigs.

The artist sat her on a carved bishop's chair, spread her olive-coloured dress so its folds fell heavily to the floor. He wanted her to wear a choker fitted high at the throat in place of the string of rubies which now hung below the *décolletage*, so he unclasped it and wrapped it five times around her neck, to form a band of crimson, noting how well the red complemented the olive of her dress. He pulled a yellow lily from a nearby vase and placed this on her lap, and was pleased with the juxtaposed colours of yellow, deep red and green.

First he asked her to look directly at him, because he wanted to catch her dark eyes, but then he changed his idea for the composition and told her to look behind him, so that it would seem there was another person present: an invisible other.

Theodora sat for him in this position for days, fatigued by having to keep still and tiring of the smells of linseed oil and paint, wanting to be with her husband as he walked the estate checking on the orchards and dairy. She grew irritated watching the artist squeeze colours from small pouches of pigskin, then stare at them, now facing the window, now turning from it, as he let light and then shadow play on the paints. The velvet dress was hot; no breeze came up from the land and through the window to cool her.

The portraitist did not speak as he worked. Sometimes he would stare at her for long stretches, and then barely look at her at all. His brush strokes were vigorous; his mixing of the colours agitated. At other times he would walk away from the easel and look at the canvas, with his arms folded across his chest, or his hands in the pockets of his smock, from far across the room or from a corner. He neither ate nor drank while he painted, but at the end of each day went down to the kitchen where he was served a good meal and a glass of mead. Here he would light his pipe and draw deeply at the hot tobacco.

When it was finished the painting was framed and hung in the dining hall, behind Theodora's place, so her husband could look at her and also up at her image when they sat together at table. It captured her strong features, but also a longing, for in looking beyond the artist while he painted her, and in focusing on the tapestry that hung on the far wall behind him, her thoughts had taken her away from the present, into her past and the apothecary's room.

★ ★ ★

The nobleman travelled regularly, and a pattern to their lives was soon set. He returned from his journeys with various consignments of gold, jewels and artefacts: antique cameos; weavings and carpets, scrolls, fabrics as fine as skin; precious stones; leather pouches filled with rare dyes of rich and exotic colours — metallic blues, sea greens, rusted reds, umbers, russets. He brought back beautifully blown and decorated glassware: bowls and goblets of colours filigreed with gold and coppers trapped within them, and in which light seemed to pause and ponder its passage through the exquisite workings of master glassmakers. With all these treasures came also new smells, aromas of faraway places, of smoke, of hessian. There came exotic fragrances of spices and barks, and the odours of cured skins; all transported into the castle from lands far beyond.

All the nobleman's newly acquired treasures would be laid out for display, first for his wife to admire (and take whatever she chose) and then for those who bought from him. He would hold something back for the Queen, and it became his wife's task to choose what would be fitting. 'What would the Queen fancy, my beloved? A green opal? But put aside one smaller than yours, of course. Or a cluster of sapphire? Though keep the deeper-coloured one, let her have the lighter, I pray,' he teased, and they would laugh.

Not only jewellers and merchants came, but also collectors of antiquities, and agents acting on behalf of nobles and foreign royals. The hallway and showroom would be busy with people; at night the castle burned with lamplight.

Leonardo would stay at home a few weeks, sometimes a few months. In this time he would draw maps of new regions, or update depictions of known territories. He duplicated all his work, keeping one copy for himself and rolling a second into a vellum casing that he dispatched to the Queen in the capital, with her chosen treasure.

Then he would begin preparing for his next journey. This he would plan according to what was ordered by merchants and dealers. If nothing specific were asked for, he would decide on journeys to new, unknown territories.

He would set off just as morning broke the night, with his mounted men, provisioned for basic self-sufficiency, and from her balcony Theodora would watch him make his way down the road and away to his distant and often unnamed destination.

While her husband was away, Theodora ate her meals alone, in the great dining hall, though Halla sat under the window waiting for her. She was served wholesome meals of meats, fruits and vegetables grown and reared on the estate and presented to her on delicately patterned blue porcelain plates with silver cutlery; sometimes gilt-edged or fine white china bore her food. She drank from crystal goblets. Between meals she wandered about the estate — perhaps she would sit with the beekeeper and watch as he strained honey, or smoked a hive to extract sheets of golden, dripping comb while bees clustered upon his black hands and arms. She would go to the chicken runs; or to the pastures and watch the calves butting at their mothers' teats. Sometimes she just sat in the walled flower garden, which during spring was a mass of white roses, white lilies, white jasmine, white agapanthus, white gardenia, white oleander and white jonquils.

Theodora would be drawn to the kitchen when bread was baking, or when fruit conserves were being boiled and bottled, enjoying the wholesome smells. The cook would cut thick slices of bread for her and spread them generously with deep yellow butter and rich red jams. Then she would sit on the bench just outside the kitchen door and enjoy this modest fare, her thoughts drifting back to her previous life, to its order and simplicity, to the sound of nuns walking down the corridors to chapel, their long rosaries rattling, their habits sighing. She would reminisce upon the convent kitchen, which was also a place of comfort though it carried different smells, of bean broths and porridge. She wondered who now helped the apothecary gently crush dried herbs; who helped her macerate leaves and roots and flowers; who sealed the bottled tinctures and labelled them.

Theodora often sat on her balcony. If the north-west wind blew it would bring to her the sounds of the town below the escarpment

— the cries of vendors on market days, the baying of dogs, the calls of children at play, the noises of common life. She wondered about the people who lived there, and whether there was anyone who might befriend her, should she go down. She thought about her husband's Nubian servants, and about Halla, and how it was for them to live here, so far from home, and reflected on why they had chosen not to return after their master had granted them their freedom.

★ ★ ★

In the early years of their marriage, when Leonardo travelled Theodora would be engulfed by feelings of loneliness, and fears that he might never come home again. She imagined him dying on a far-off road somewhere, being attacked by animals or pirates, his horse losing footing and tumbling with him down a precipitous mountain path. Such images played before her and left her a widow, alone in their castle, even more alone than she was now, without a grave to lay flowers upon, without ever knowing what had become of her husband.

There was no longer need to practise the arts she had been taught at the convent. She did not spin, nor weave, nor sew, for this the servants did. It was not necessary to gather plants and extract their essences and oils, or to use her apothecial knowledge here. Anyway, she did not want to make tinctures and remedies, for this reminded her of her past. If there was illness, the doctor was summoned from the town, one who did not rely on herbal preparations but who used purging and blood-letting in his treatments.

So she just waited for her husband to return, staring out from the escarpment, her glance tracing the road which wound its way out from the estate along the river, through the town, then away towards the horizon. There lay a world unknown to her, the places where her husband journeyed or tarried, traded and collected; the places she knew about only through the stories he told, the artefacts he brought back and the maps he drew.

Sometimes, when Leonardo was away, she would go to his quarters and lie on his cotton mattress, burying her face into it to find the smell of him and the trace oils of his skin. She would lie on her back, looking up at the painted ceiling, at the angels playing flageolets, and she would think about babies and wonder why her husband did not properly consummate their marriage, why he stopped her hands from exploring his body, keeping them at his breast, at that beaded scar, and in his mass of silken hair. Was her humble upbringing among sisters of a holy order a stigma which his nobility could not transcend? she wondered. But if it was, she reasoned, he would not have fetched her. Surely he could have chosen anyone he wanted to be his wife.

In time, Theodora accepted the pattern of their lives, and settled into its order.

⋆ ⋆ ⋆

The nobleman was twenty-five years older than his wife, a man who, born to great wealth, had had the time to study and pursue his own interests. He read extensively from his good collection of books and scrolls, among which were ancient, leather-bound treatises on the origins of life, and its nature. Though he did business with many people, and was cartographer to the Queen, he had only one friend — a Jew exiled from Syria and living in Egypt. He did not socialize with other nobles, and never attended the royal court, something the Queen did not pressure him to do, for she had come to respect and understand his chosen solitude. She valued his services as cartographer above those of all

45

her subjects, and made no demand of him save that he continue to explore unknown regions and map them for her archive alone.

At home, Leonardo chose to live a private, secluded life, farming and tending his property. It was generally accepted that his elected isolation had to do with his grief at the deaths of his twin and father. In fact he found court life shallow and petty, and so allowed a false impression of his eccentricity and introversion to persist.

He was sensitive to the fact that he was inflicting his chosen solitude upon his young wife and, concerned at her loneliness when he was away, he drew her into his world, encouraging her to read his books. He gave her the notebooks of his travels, in which careful record was made of the peoples he encountered, the geographical wonders he saw, the minerals he discovered and the plants, animals and insects he found himself amongst. His writings were not elaborate or lengthy, but short, precise, decorative vignettes. Sometimes only a line or two described what he had seen or experienced. He took with him quills and inks and made fine sketches in the margins of his recordings. With these journals Theodora could retrace his steps, and journey too, vicariously, to remote exotic places.

When he was home, she always stayed at

his side, sitting with him at his maps, watching him depict with ink pens a newly discovered river, a mountain range or the place of a water source. In time he taught her this skill, and how to draw to scale and to meticulously transcribe from his sketches and measurements. Once she was accomplished, it was her copy of each new map, signed by her in the corner, that he rolled into vellum and sent to the Queen.

'I am married to the Royal Cartographer,' Leonardo teased, and they would laugh together as they worked with pen and ink over their depictions of his journeys. He taught her how to account for and balance the money he made selling treasure; how to pay the labourers, both in money and in produce; and how to dispatch to his cousin, the Queen's confessor, an annual tithe in terms of his father's will. Theodora helped him count out the heavy gold coins with which he paid his riders after a journey. He showed her how to determine the age and value of Persian and Chinese carpets, of paintings, of cut jewels. She learnt to tell fake gold and silver from the real, merely by feeling their weight in her palm.

Donna Theodora, in her castle, without the smells of dust or heat, without sensual participation in those of earth's components which she so accurately mapped (jungle, waterfall, abyss, savannah), was like the artists of a later period, who drew pictures of wilderness and newly conquered territory from the descriptions and sketches brought home by intrepid explorers. Like her, these artists had never experienced the hardship and terror of travel, but only its wondrous description, which they translated on to paper and canvas. Like her, they had no direct knowledge of colours muted and softened by dry red dusts; had never heard the sounds of wind passing through trees laden with giant dry pods, so the trees seemed to sing. Thus their paintings were as still and silent as all those others which hung in academies and galleries. Only experienced travellers gazing upon them would hear the song and sigh of wilderness.

When not busy with their maps and books and money, Leonardo and Theodora walked together across the farmlands, as he checked the orchards and the drying sheds, enquired about the crops or calves. If the sun was too hot, a Nubian servant would hold a parasol above her. The nobleman would send a gardener up to the kitchen to order refreshments. Then he and his wife would sit in the pagoda enjoying meats and breads and wine, while the sounds of the farmland wove themselves into a melody of contentment.

They ate three times a day in the dining hall; they drank pressed fruit juices mid-afternoon. In the evenings she undid his plait and brushed his long hair as he leant back on his chair so it hung down, thick and black and shining. They read to each other, from his notebooks and from certain volumes in his library written by other travellers and explorers, and they discussed all the world's knowledge that had come their way. He thought she should learn to ride, so each morning the groom was tasked with leading her around the stableyard, until she was able to trot, canter and then gallop alongside her husband through the farmlands.

Sometimes they rode beyond the castle grounds, with a basket of food, to the ruins of a Roman town that littered the area, and they would sit on fallen statues and pillars or on the aqueduct to eat. Once, he found old glass beads, which the wind had exposed, lying in a line, their thread rotted away. 'They might have been dropped yesterday, so perfect are they,' Leonardo said, handing them to her, and she held them up to the light and marvelled at the tiny bubbles of air trapped within them. They collected from among the ruins shards of pottery, the handles of jugs, the elegantly curved bases of amphorae, and spoke, under the orange African sun, about the coming and going of empires.

One evening, sitting beside the fallen, broken statue of a discus thrower (they had named him Achilles because his ankle was smashed) and watching the stars emerge from the softening daylight into the encroaching night, he took her in his arms and said, 'The Queen has written to say she is well pleased that you have become such an accomplished cartographer. She is delighted that there are now two of us working for her, though she cautioned me not to take you travelling into the wilderness and the unknown, lest something harm you.

'Even though you don't travel with me, how easily you could step into my shoes and take my place. You can ride and keep finances and weigh gold as well as I can.'

'Indeed yes, but I prefer my soft slippers to your boots,' she replied, and they laughed.

'How we have grown to love and need each other,' he said, kissing her mouth. 'I cannot imagine my life without you.'

'Nor I mine without you, dear husband.'

★   ★   ★

Leonardo Capelutto's friend, the elderly Syrian Jew, was a mathematician called

Balthazar. He visited at least once a year, usually at one of the equinoxes — summer and winter — and the nobleman tried to pass through Alexandria whenever his journeys took him eastward. The two men had grown close to one another despite their difference in age. They explored all new knowledge together, exchanged books and scrolls, debated fiercely, probed the sciences and surveyed the cosmos. Theodora was drawn into their relationship warmly and without question. They shared with her their excitement of new discoveries; they taught her to challenge the accepted order of knowledge, to question the prevailing small-mindedness of the Church. From them she learnt that the age in which they lived was a dark one, hamstrung by ignorance and bled to near-death by bigotry.

Theodora grew to love Balthazar. Something about him reminded her of the apothecary, and she came to imagine that if she had had a real father it would have been someone like him.

When he visited, he would arrive at the outskirts of the town on mule-back with a young servant, whom he would send up to the castle with word of his arrival. A wagon would come down to fetch him. Fatigued by his journey, the old man would lie for a day or two in the guest room set aside for him until he recovered his strength. A servant would be allotted to him, to bathe and oil him and to massage his age-withered muscles, while his own servant, an Egyptian boy, would join the beekeeper at his work and be rewarded with honeycomb to suck.

When Theodora first met Balthazar, soon after her marriage to the nobleman, the old man complained of an eye infection and lamented that he walked with difficulty, for his bones were old and his joints arthritic. She noted his thick-knuckled fingers, the curled silver hair under his skullcap, his white beard and long brown kaftan, a circle of red cloth sewn on to the shoulder, which her husband later told her publicly marked him as a Jew and which he was obliged to wear when travelling through their country.

On that first night, after they had eaten well and drunk a Portuguese wine that Balthazar had brought with him, he presented her with an Egyptian-faience cosmetic bowl, saying simply, 'It comes from a pharaoh's tomb, and I give it to you to celebrate your marriage.'

Once the servants had been dismissed and the castle doors closed, the nobleman led his young wife and their visitor to his room, which he bolted from the inside. He then unlocked the oak door and, with oil lamp in hand, led them up the spiral steps. She heard the old man labour behind her, and watched the darkness of the stairwell yield to the light of the lamp.

The stairs led to a small circular room with a wide balcony all the way around it at the highest point of the castle. At its entrance was a small silver *mezuzza*, which the two men touched. There was no moon. Leonardo extinguished the lamp. In the utter darkness of night the stars seemed like *argentum* milk spilt across deep blue velvet.

Balthazar had with him a slim leather case, from which he took a telescope. He handed this to Leonardo, who put it to his eye, pointing it upwards to the sky. After a while he gave it to his wife, showing her how to hold it against one eye and close the other. She looked towards the spread of white across the sky and, startled at the sudden rushing proximity of the stars, stumbled backwards. The old man chuckled, and her husband laughed, steadying her as she looked through the glass again.

Through the hours of the night they surveyed the firmament, taking turns with the telescope, watching the stars and planets on their journey down to the edge of the earth. Balthazar and Leonardo shared with her their secret knowledge: 'We are stargazers,' said her husband. 'We are privy to the forbidden.'

'The stars are not lanterns and lamps suspended in the night sky as is generally believed,' added Balthazar. 'Nor is the sky a great dark cloth, nor a moving dome with small holes cut into it through which shines the light of God from the heavens beyond, giving the appearance of stars.'

'The stars are in fact burning masses, as is our sun,' said Leonardo.

'Yes, our sun is a star,' said Balthazar. 'But more than this, the earth is not fixed in its position, nor are the visible planets. Instead of being motionless, they move around the sun, and also upon their own axes.

'Although they move, they do not fly away from each other but are held together in suspension. Nor do they fall from the heavens, but remain as though chained to the sun. There is some mysterious holding force that keeps them in place.'

'It is a dance, above and around us,' said Leonardo. 'A silent planetary dance.' While he spoke, his voice took her thoughts to the sound of prayer that laced perpetually through the convent, holding everything in place. And to the sound of the reed flutes and drums which the Nubians played and which seemed to net the sounds of the night — crickets, night-birds, wind.

'Perhaps,' Balthazar postulated, 'the deep darkness between the stars is not just black barrenness. Perhaps, though this emptiness is not visible, it is none the less tangible. Perhaps, but who would ever know?, the darkness between the stars is black matter held in position by the same mysterious holding force that keeps the planets in place.'

When the first rim of dawn red touched the horizon, and the stars began to acquiesce to the light of morning, Leonardo told his wife never to speak of what he and Balthazar had disclosed to her. 'Stargazing is punishable by death. The Church would have us believe that the earth is at the centre of the universe, so hold safe this knowledge we have shared with you.'

Later in the day she asked one of the Nubians to gather for her the leaves of *Symphytum* and the flowers of *Euphrasia*. Then she explained to the cook how to make up a tincture from the flowers, for the old man to bathe his eyes, and a tea from the leaves to relieve the inflammation in his joints.

Balthazar stayed with them for a month. Each night, after they had eaten, the three would lock the castle, unlock the oak door, then mount the spiral stairs and view the heavens.

'You must go about your life always looking up at the sky,' Balthazar told her on the eve of his departure home, when explaining how the beautiful Venus grew from crescent to fullness, as did the earth's moon, 'for it will keep you humbly in your place. It will remind you that you are very small, and that all about you is magnitude.

'You must live your life as though you dwell in a sacred holy place, in a shrine; always be in awe; always pay full respect to existence. In that way you will live a truly religious life, without need of prayerbooks and churches, for you will be within a temple all the time, with its roof of stars and its walls the divine masterpiece of earth.'

★   ★   ★

Thus Donna Theodora Capelutto became a traveller in her own right; one who knew of three types of journeying, shared with her by three types of voyagers.

The inner journey, the journey into the soul, the one the nuns travelled day in and day out, was charted by the beads of rosaries and the repetition of prayer. The nuns had all entered the holy order as young girls, virgins with knowledge only of childhood, in whom true womanhood would remain a sealed, unbroken mystery. They had spent years in the same rhythm of life, the same cadence of prayer, so their journeys into the interior of the soul, through which they had escorted Theodora during her life with them, were light, glacial, beautiful and harboured no ill, carrying a promise of eternal life.

The outer journey, the journey across the external landscape of earth, the one that her husband voyaged, which took into account mountains and seas and valleys, and through which he led her vicariously, was charted by his own maps and journals as well as those of earlier travellers; by legends and hearsay. Measuring instruments, compasses, astrolabes and sextants brought order to the vast terrestrial territories he entered, but this order did not tame wilderness or harness danger. All his journeys to the exterior, in opening doors to backdrops of untold beauty, carried the risk of death.

Balthazar's journey among the stars, beyond all that which was known, was charted neither by prayer nor by voyaging but by observation and mathematical speculation. The old man drew back the curtain that the Church had drawn across the firmament and revealed a titanic but finely tuned mechanism, a balanced and precise collaboration between numberless moving celestial bodies, with the earth merely an infinitesimally small piece of the whole. He had no maps of the extraterrestrial territory he ventured into; there were few earlier astronomers whose courses he could follow. His journeys into the beyond opened the very heavens and challenged the described order of the universe. Following him, Theodora ventured into celestial territories that the Church deemed belonged to it and God alone. These journeys too carried the threat of death.

★　　★　　★

Balthazar and Leonardo were not alone in their knowledge of and speculations on the nature of the universe. They were two among a small group of learned men and scholars who lived in various Mediterranean countries and who observed the movements of celestial bodies in relation to the earth. They confirmed that the earth was round (though this had already been grudgingly accepted by the Ecclesiastical Court) and also surmised that the universe was infinite, without boundary, and that it was filled with numberless galaxies and vast collections of stars. Balthazar had collated their various theses on the cosmos, printing and binding them for wider distribution.

For many years, the old man had travelled between the northern and southern hemispheres, to study and compare the different views of the night sky. He documented the infinitesimally distant smudges in the black southern sky that seemed to have broken away from the earth's galaxy and that he surmised to be collections of billions of suns. (In a later century they would be named the Magellanic Clouds.)

Balthazar also regularly visited a friend in Florence, one Galileo Galilei, who had perfected the Chinese method of grinding optical lenses, and made telescopes with which to view the night sky. He had given one to Balthazar. This friend had written a treatise on the nature of the tides, and the way in which the earth's moon controlled their movement. He documented the dark spots that crept continuously across the face of the sun.

Balthazar and Leonardo had met years before, in the crowded market of the Coptic quarter in Cairo, where each was looking through old maps and navigational charts. They were drawn to one another, the shy Jew in his kaftan and embroidered skullcap, and the confident, upright traveller who wore a coat of embossed leather, his long hair plaited and hanging down his back.

They decided to share their accommodation, for they had much to discuss and compare. The two spent the next few weeks drinking mint tea at meeting houses; or sitting on the flat roof of their lodging, watching the stars and eating pitta bread filled with lamb and bulgar that they had bought from street vendors. They discussed the nature of creation and the mysterious order of the cosmos. They drank the pressed juice of tamarind and sweetened lemon cordial; they ate sugared orange peel and almonds.

Their friendship was forged under the Egyptian sky and it was here that they agreed to meet at least twice a year, at the nobleman's home.

On their last night together, on the roof, in the light of the full moon and a lantern, the nobleman took off his shirt and showed his companion the scar which cut across his breast. 'Look upon me; look at how I am marked,' he had said bitterly, reaching for Balthazar's hands and placing them upon the line of stitches, holding them there. Balthazar gazed into Leonardo's fine-looking face, and his eyes filled with tears as he took his young friend in his arms, holding him against his own body, against the smoothness of his robe. Then he bent to pick up Leonardo's shirt and put it back on him, not to conceal the torturous look of the scar, not to protect himself from its rude sore sight, not because it felt improper to look upon this testimony of some horrendous injury. He covered his companion as one might wrap a child to protect it from the elements. It was an act of love.

Later, when they sat watching the white moon set and the red sun rise through the ruddy pearled sky of dawn (for they had not slept that night), and after the young nobleman had told Balthazar what had befallen him and how he had come to be so maimed, Balthazar mulled, 'Life inscribes itself upon us all, in one way or another, whether by treacherous outward welts and scars such as yours, or by inscriptions upon our very hearts and souls. We all of us carry the captions of our lives upon our faces and bodies, within and without, for others to read. Who is to know why some have their story carved upon them in a more brutal way than others do? Who is to know whether it is the hand of God writing, or whether we ourselves are the artisans and artists, inventing and engraving our own story, our own histories, into our physical forms?

'Perhaps, in the end, we are mere books, mere bindings of parchment or cuneiform-covered slabs of stone, each a story with which, collectively, we make up the story of humankind, encompassing all our brutalities and loves.

'I am filled with sorrow that your life's tale has so savagely marked you. Would that it had been a love sonnet inscribed upon your brow; or a map of the heavens sketched around your eyes.'

When it was time to go, when the nobleman's horse was saddled and ready, Balthazar embraced him and said, 'Like stars! We are nothing more than stars, marking a way, marking a passageway through emptiness, nothing more. Only our own death should stop us in our movement, and even then we might take another form, to continue with what it is we are to express. Live your life, my dear friend. Live, marry, let not what has befallen you hinder you in any way.'

Balthazar watched Leonardo mount, then stood back and waved, calling out, 'I will join you for the next eclipse of the moon! Have ready a good meal and I will bring a fine wine!'

'I shall await you, and my heart shall be filled with joy to see you again,' said the nobleman, saluting then riding off slowly through the crowded market, heading for the western gate, where the water sellers stood.

★   ★   ★

One night, a year or so after Theodora had met Balthazar, the wind brought from the town the shouts of a crowd and the sound of shots bringing the mass to order. She watched from her balcony, grasping the rail as, in the distance, the lights of three small fires suddenly burst into huge gouts of flame.

Tortured screams, so horrible they contorted all other sound, cut the night. The cries reached an unbearable pitch, then they seemed to explode into an infinitely drawn out soprano of agony, before collapsing into deadly silence. The fires reached their frenzied zenith, and then burned steadily.

Church bells rang. The wind carried the sweet, sickly smell of burnt flesh and smoke, the sounds of chanting and sung prayer, and a coarse white ash which settled everywhere. But this was not the prayer of compassion and adoration that Theodora had grown up with. It was a different form of prayer, one she did not know; one that frightened her. Her hands were locked to the rail; she could not move away. Halla came to fetch her inside, but could not undo her mistress's grip, so hurried down to call the nobleman.

Leonardo held Theodora's shoulders and turned her to face him, holding and soothing her as she shook with weeping. He led her indoors and motioned to Halla to close the balcony door and draw the curtains. Then he sat with his young wife on her bed.

'They are burning people condemned as heathens, condemned to death by the Office of the Inquisition,' he explained. 'And books. They are burning books. This is the white ash of condemned knowledge falling everywhere.'

'What are heathens?' she asked.

'The Church despises more than mere stargazing. It vilifies Jews and Moors as well. Jews are accused of all manner of untrue things — of spreading the plague, of sacrificing children, of using Christian blood to make their Sabbath bread. There have always been prohibitions placed on them: they are heavily taxed, and they are forced to live in their own quarters, apart from Christians. There is constant pressure on them either to convert to Christianity or to leave the kingdom.

'I imagine tonight's executions have something to do with these persecutions, though I don't know why they were carried out here. These killings by fire are generally conducted in the larger towns or the capital. I suppose it is a means of spreading terror. I'm sorry you witnessed this; sorry to have sullied your innocence, which I have always sought to protect.

'I should tell you now that my cousin,

Cardinal Uriel, the Queen's confessor, is the Inquisitor. It is he who would have condemned the wretches to death, he who would have ordered the confiscation of any written work of new knowledge, or knowledge that challenges what is acceptable to the Church. I heard that he is travelling through this region and staying at the abbey down below the town.'

'Your cousin is the Inquisitor?' Theodora asked, drawing a deep breath. 'Does he know about your library, and that we watch the stars? Does he know about Balthazar? Would he not judge and condemn us as well?'

'Even though he envies and despises me, both for my personal wealth and my fiscal power, I am not afraid of him and nor need you be. We might be cousins, and we might both work for the Queen, but friends and confidants we are not. So he knows nothing of my interests. Anyway, he has not been in my home for years. We have, in fact, not seen or spoken to each other since my father's death. And before that we hardly spent time together, for he is some ten years older than I and was reared by Dominicans, in a monastery.'

Hours later, only three red glows marked the areas where the conflagrations had consumed that which had so eagerly sustained their flames. The wind had dropped.

The sick smell it had delivered still hung in the air, and seemed trapped in Theodora's hair and on her skin. She thought she could taste it and was nauseated.

Leonardo and Theodora lay on her bed, she in his arms, unable to sleep, he telling her stories of places far away, to take her mind from the new and terrible knowledge that had been delivered to her. Then he began to explain:

'We are the great-grandsons of a Jewess, my cousin and I. But, whereas I am not troubled by the blood in my veins, he despises what he believes taints his. Our great-grandfather, Lorenzo Capelutto, married a Jewish woman, one from a wealthy family named Loyola, who brought with her an immense dowry with which he was able to settle debts. It was a strategic marriage, and not uncommon in those days, though I believe they came to respect and love each other as the years went by. She was baptized on the morning of their wedding and never more practised her Jewish faith. My grandfather and then my father after him used the wealth they inherited wisely, trading in exotic goods, as I still do.

'After the death of my twin and my father, my cousin believed he would share my father's wealth with me. By that stage he was already well positioned in the Church hierarchy, and very powerful.

'He wanted to use my father's money to build a monastery, to set up his own order. But nothing of consequence was left to him. My father willed everything to my twin and me, but as my twin had died the entire estate became mine, with only an annual stipend for my cousin, which I am at liberty to cancel if I so wish. But I continue to pay it. Even though it is a fairly large fee, I hardly feel its loss, for my own fortune is considerable. By paying it without argument, I do not provoke him or give him reason to trouble me.'

'Tell me,' she said: 'why did your father leave so little to your cousin? Why only a stipend and not a part of the estate? Why was everything willed to you and your twin?'

'Because of his hatred of the Jews — even as a young priest he embraced a fervent anti-Semitism. My father died before my cousin's rise to the position of Inquisitor, so he never knew the extent of this hatred; he judged him on his youthful behaviour alone. Remember, my father's grandmother was a converted Jewess. Though she lived an outwardly Catholic life, she told him Hebrew stories when he was a boy, and whispered Judaic prayers to him late at night. He knew to be secretive. He handed the prayers on to my twin and me. We too knew never to express these prayers publicly, but only in our hearts. Though we knew nothing of the old rituals, our souls were, as mine still is, Jewish.

'But my father was a kind man, not a vindictive, punitive person. Though he disliked my cousin intensely, he recognized many of the factors that made him who he was. He was brought up by Dominican monks and groomed for priesthood from an early age. Under the Dominicans, my cousin was subjected to certain cruelties which embedded themselves within him, so he came to believe they were normal to life.

'Using his cunning — he was born sly, of this there is no doubt — and his noble birth, he worked his way up into the royal court, where he is positioned today and where he strongly influences the Queen. Over the years his power has grown, as has his liking for comfort and wealth.

'He was permitted to visit us occasionally as a young man, in the few years before he took his monastic vows, and at such times displayed coarse behaviour. He molested one of the dairy girls. He forced himself upon her — she was a mere child. When my father heard of this, he stopped Uriel visiting altogether. He willed the stipend not for any concern or care of my cousin, but because Uriel was his sister's only son, and thus my father's only nephew.

'But enough now of him. See how quiet you have grown, and how serious. Clear him from your thoughts. Come with me; let us go up to the viewing tower and see what the heavens have to show us tonight. Balthazar wrote to tell me of a comet in the southern hemisphere, huge and visible. We might see it through our eyeglass, though for us, in our hemisphere, it will appear very small.'

Outside their cottages the Nubians sat together, the cries of dying men and the falling ash stirring memories within them of burning villages and slain elders, of their capture into slavery, of iron collars and chained feet. They stayed up till dawn, not daring to close their eyes or sleep, not daring to enter a darkness through which galloped the demonic steeds of slave traders and the looters of tranquillity.

★ ★ ★

'Tell me about the Queen, to whom the maps I draw are sent,' said Theodora. 'I imagine her like my holy mother in the convent, clothed in simple white and black. Someone kind and good, someone who gathers seeds and smells of herbs.'

Leonardo laughed out loud and exclaimed,

'Clothed in simple black and white! As a nun! The Queen!'

They were at the Roman ruins, lying amid seeding grasses and yellow wild flowers.

'Tell me! Tell me! Why laugh you so?' she asked, shaking him playfully. 'How is she in appearance?'

'The Queen, my sweet love, is dressed from hair to foot in jewels,' he said. 'She sits upon chairs of gold and sleeps on a bed inlaid with ivory. She owns nothing unadorned nor simple. All who attend to her are clothed in finery, always bowing and bending to her and sweeping the floor in deference. She eats from plates of gold and drinks from goblets studded with pearls. Our home, sumptuous as it is, when viewed beside hers is plain indeed.

'Do you want to know who holds and reads your maps? Shall I tell you about her? Come, walk with me to the theatre seats and I will tell you all I know, for we were children together. And I should not laugh, for once we played and rode, here among these very ruins, long ago.'

Leonardo helped Theodora to her feet, dusted the grasses from her dress and hair and led her through the colonnades to the amphitheatre where they sat as the afternoon sun played upon carved stone.

'She was born with a lame left leg and disfigured foot, small and bent in upon itself,' he said. 'Surgeons and physicians were called from far and wide to attend to her as she grew, to lengthen the leg and straighten the foot, to make her look agreeable and walk properly. But all they did was inflict pain and suffering; she became an impossible wretch, always screaming and demanding her way with everything.

'Once, when my father was attending court, her screams rang throughout the palace as surgeons stretched the leg against a cane of gold and strapped the foot upward, believing to straighten it. My father, wise and courageous, asked to see the little princess, and when he saw what the physicians were up to, deeming them buffoons, he suggested to the King that he allow the royal child to come away from the palace and to live in the country with us.

'The King let her come, and she arrived with a retinue of servants and attendants and coaches full of trunks. But my father sent them all back and kept the little girl with us, growing up without pomposity.

'At first my twin and I hated her, for she was spoilt and always wanted her own way with everything. We would run away from her and hide, and laugh as she stumbled along on

71

her club foot trying to follow us, and we ridiculed her when she fell over, and never helped her to get up, so she would lie there like a beetle on its back, crying. But in time she stopped behaving as though we were her servants and subjects, she stopped trying to force her will upon us. So we let her come into our world. My father had a carpenter make her a splint of rosewood, lined with silk and leather, with a little compartment to hold the foot, and raised to give the leg more length.

'We taught her to balance properly when she ran, and to ride like a boy, so she grew up wild as we were, country children who enjoyed the simple pleasure of the outdoors. We did not call her Majesty, or Highness, but named her Maru, from her name Marie-Ursula.'

'Did she ever go home?' asked Theodora.

'She did not want to go home,' replied Leonardo. 'But she had to, once she reached marriageable age. She was the King's only child, and heir to the throne. She had to go back to the palace to be taught to be a queen-in-waiting. Princes from foreign countries had presented their credentials to her father, and he had chosen one to marry his daughter, but she was not interested in any of the other royals. She loved only one person.'

'Whom did she love?'

'If I tell you whom she loved, I will have to tell you much else. I will have to tell you what I have kept back from you all these years.'

'Tell me.'

'Very well, but I will recount it as though it is a tale, a novella, for it happened long ago and has become but an old story in my mind, lacking resonance, put away like a book of faded pages with worn binding.

'Princess Marie-Ursula and a young nobleman were once lovers. They wanted to marry. They discovered their bodies here among the Roman ruins. They kissed and held hands and made love among the vestiges of where Latin youths must once have done the same, and where dramatists once acted out scenes of passion and enchantment. They play-acted, down there on the stage, she as Eurydice and he Orpheus; or she Thisbe and he Pyramus. They loved each other as only the very young love, innocently and believing in nothing else but themselves. They thought they would marry, restore this ruin to a former glory and live here for ever, going to court only to play at pomp and ceremony, but always staying in this wild and magic place where they could play at romantic dramas and be for ever happy together.'

Leonardo grew silent. Now the carved

stones of the amphitheatre were a deep red-grey as the setting sun darkened them; and shadows stood among them, like phantoms from the past coming forward to reclaim a place no longer theirs.

Theodora watched his fine profile as he told his tale.

'But the young nobleman and his twin decided to go on a long adventure to test their skills, for they were both courageous riders and travellers. They went alone on a journey of daring and valour. They told everyone that they were going to the glass workers of Venice, to buy beads for trade along the east coast. ('I will bring you back beads of red gold,' the young nobleman told his betrothed.) But instead he and his twin went into unknown territories, where savages ruled. They were gone a long time; it seemed they would never return. Scouts were sent out to Venice, the glass workers were questioned. Innkeepers and tavern proprietors were interrogated. But no one had seen them. It was believed they would never return — it was thought they had been killed.

'In time, the King urged his young daughter to forget the one she loved, to marry another. But she refused to believe that he would not come back. She would stand at the edge of the sea, waiting, watching the waves crash in against the shore, looking out to the far distance for the sails of a ship bearing him home. Finally the King came to fetch her back to the palace, where she continued to wait faithfully, believing always she would see him again, rejecting all offers of marriage.

'And indeed the young nobleman did eventually come back. But he returned without his twin, and broken in body and soul. They had ventured south, into the desert regions, *terra incognita*, where few civilized men had ever gone and returned from. In that barely charted wilderness, the two were attacked by savages. The sibling was brutally slain while the young nobleman's body was mutilated, and his spirit crushed. Once he returned home, he was no longer the laughing young person he had been, but one morose and dark; not only because of his injuries, but because he had left his twin's ruined body in the desert. It had never come home for proper burial.

'The Crown Princess came to him as soon as she heard he was back. But he would not let her see him. He locked his room and left her to cry and wail outside, and when she did eventually enter his room, when she commanded a servant to force the door, her lover remained concealed behind his bed curtains, under his linens, refusing to show his face and telling her to go from his life, to marry a prince and forget him. He abused her and spoke foully to her, behaving like a madman, in order that she should go.

'Her father came again to fetch her and forced her to return to the palace. But before she left she opened her bodice and cut a square of lace from the undergarment that covered her breasts, and placed this beside her lover's bed. And then every year, on the anniversary of his homecoming, she sent him another square, until he had the whole garment, in pieces in an ebony box, her whole life cut up, symbolically, into small bits.

'The Crown Princess continued to write to her lover and plead, hoping that when he strengthened he would change his mind and marry her. She sent an emissary once. He stood at the nobleman's curtained bedside and spoke her message aloud. The emissary intoned, 'I speak for Crown Princess Marie-Ursula: We have both broken bodies, it matters not. Our love is strong enough, deep enough to overcome all. You mended my spirit when I was a child; let me now mend yours.' But still the nobleman refused her. In the end she had to accept that she had lost him. Thus she never married, but took on the role of a widow. When the King died, she turned to the Church, laying herself at the

mercy of the nobleman's cousin, the Dominican, who had been cardinal and religious
administrator to the King. He became her
confessor and manipulated her fine spirit to
serve his own.

'You may think that the young nobleman
was completely heartless, but he was not. He
understood her suffering. But he could not
face her with his broken body. In time, he
began to travel, so as to be away; and when he
was home, he filled his lonely hours by
drawing maps. When she one day learnt of
this, she sent word that she wanted the maps,
so he began to make copies for her, allowing
her to trace his life with those charts, allowing
her to follow his life as though on horseback
with him.

'You see,' he said, turning to face his wife,
'once the nobleman regained his spirit he did
respond to her, to Maru, his old friend. Only
he could never marry her, indeed could never
look into her eyes again.

'When the King died, and Marie-Ursula
was made Queen, the nobleman did not go to
her coronation. Instead, he lay in this Roman
theatre, staring up at the sky from morning
until it filled with stars and then emptied as
the sun rose after them. He wept here, on
these very stones.

'But enough now of this cruel tale,' said

Leonardo, standing up. He ran his palms across his chest, along the line of scars, feeling them through the cloth of his shirt, saying, 'Come! Is there food left in our basket? Have we finished the wine? Shall we eat beside the fallen head of Diana? Or dine with our Achilles? Who shall host us as we feast?'

But Theodora held him back, challenging, 'You are that nobleman, are you not? This is not a tale from a printed volume. This is your story.'

'Yes, I am that nobleman,' confirmed her husband. 'And the story is true indeed.'

'Why have you never told me this?'

'I am telling you now.'

'What did she say, when you married me? What did the Queen say? Was she not angry? Surely, surely she must hate me!'

'By the time I married you, many years had passed by. She was already Queen. She knew I would never be able to be her consort, could never live a life at court. I asked her permission, before I fetched you from the convent, and she replied that it gave her great joy to know that I would no longer be alone, but that I would have someone to love. I went to the palace to ask her; I rode on my own, and we met privately, with none of her ministers and without her confessor present.

'It was she who signed our marriage certificate, and she signed it 'Maru', so I knew how much she still cared for me. I will show it to you when we get back; in fact you may have it, to keep in your casket of jewels.

'No, the Queen does not hate you, my dear one. She is pleased that I have you. You have never met her, but you can count on her being as loyal to you as she is to me.'

They walked back to the colonnades and here he poured wine and she broke bread and cheese and they ate quietly together.

'In all these years that I have been your wife, I should have known this,' said Theodora. 'I should have known that the Queen was your first love, and I but your second. I should have known about your body. Indeed, you should have shown it me.

'Show me now the scars which only my fingertips know, and tell me how you came by them. I am your wife. I should know.'

'No. I will never show you,' said her husband. 'Nor will I open the wound of my past. Let it be a measure of my love that I conceal it.'

'Has this anything to do with your never permitting me to bear children?' she whispered.

'Forgive me,' he said, then paused, silent for a short while. 'I have not purposefully denied you children. But I cannot give them.'

Leonardo undid his long plait and let his hair fall down about his shoulders. Then he took his wife in his arms and kissed her.

★ ★ ★

Outwardly, Leonardo Capelutto led a Catholic life. Mass was heard in his chapel every Sunday, he confessed regularly, was charitable and kind and was honest in all his dealings. He never blasphemed. But within himself he was a free-thinker. He had granted his Nubian slaves their liberty, soon after his father's death, because he believed that no man should own another.

Through his journeying, the nobleman had come to an understanding of life and religion that few men had. Long hours of thought and reflection while riding, his forays into the unknown and uncharted regions of the world, his experiences of other cultures and the awe which the natural, untamed wilderness aroused in him, all these led him away from the constraints of dogma and into a relationship with God which permitted him to transcend the general smallness and meanness of humankind. His experiences allowed him to step outside the known order and to question the belief structures imposed by the Church. He saw dogma for what it was — a way to control people and to stifle the natural yearnings of the human soul in its journey towards communion with the divine and its ensuing ecstasy.

Both Leonardo and Balthazar concluded that there was an underlying unity to all religious ideals. Though his friend was an orthodox Jew, and he himself a Catholic with Jewish blood in his veins, when they were together they worshipped the heavens, the movement of the celestial bodies, the precision of the universe.

Their God did not waste time standing in judgement over the petty comings and goings of people, deemed not one greater or lesser than another. Their God was the energy behind cosmic movement; the mystery within existence; the sheer magnitude of life. Their God asked not for sacrifice, nor for penance, nor for punishment, but required only homage, and this both Balthazar and Leonardo were pleased to give.

They held no belief in a devil; yet there was a devil present in their lives, one who remained concealed in the shadows, garbed in the robes of ecclesiastical hypocrisy, patiently biding his time to destroy them. The Inquisitor, Cardinal Uriel of Catalonia, knew nothing of the depth of their friendship or

81

studies, though knowledge that Leonardo received a regular singular visitor had not been difficult to obtain. Uriel knew of Balthazar's position at the university in Alexandria, and of his theses and treatises, and he was certain that the two men explored the forbidden.

The Inquisitor wanted to destroy his cousin and claim the Capelutto property as his own. To this end, he would stop at nothing. But he had to go cautiously, for he knew the Queen favoured his relative, though he had done everything in his power to poison her against him.

Although Leonardo knew the magnitude of his cousin's power, and his strong influence over the Queen, he believed his world was safe and impenetrable, that the Inquisitor would remain outside his castle walls, that he could continue to worship the god of cosmic energy without hindrance.

Part Two

Another has entered our chamber of love,
  unbidden.
This I know from the light in your eyes,
which differs from the light I kindle in
  them.
The other touches you and I know,
for my skin feels it, though I am so far
  away.
The other's lips touch yours, and I know,
for mine too sense the intruding tongue.
You are promised the earth.
Listen not,
it is not anyone's to give.
I offer you my simple love, here in the
hot open scrubland.
Come back to me.

Lamenting Figure

One day, after Leonardo and Theodora had been married some twelve years, in which time the pattern of their lives had known no disturbance but had unfolded with the predictability of the four seasons, a man rode into the estate, bringing with him a sense of something other. Pulling off his elbow-length leather gloves, lifting a plumed velvet hat from his head and bowing, he introduced himself to Theodora as Frederic Montague. He was a jeweller and purveyor of precious stones and had come from the north-east, across the sea, to ask the nobleman, who was reputed to be able to secure the most singular of treasures, to procure rare black pearls.

'My husband is away,' Donna Capelutto explained to the stranger who stood before her, upright and proud, velvet hat in hand, in the castle's large entrance hall, where warm early-afternoon sunlight poured through the stained windows. 'He has been delayed on his way home. I have word from him that he will not return before the end of the month and may even be away longer. He has been caught in a quarantined area, where there was threat of plague.

'You may leave your written order with me; I will be sure to give it to him. You say you have travelled far — perhaps you are in need of refreshment before you set off again. Should I have something prepared for you?'

'Thank you kindly, madam. Indeed, I have come a long way over a number of weeks, over the sea, from Siena in fact, and would be grateful for a glass of wine and a portion of bread. But, with due respect, and I trust you don't hear me discourteously, I would like to wait for your husband's return, to place my order into his hands in person. I need to discuss with him certain aspects of the pearls I require — their dimensions and the depth of their colour, among other things. It will hardly be worth my while to return home, only to come back again.

'Now, forgive my being so forward, madam, but would it be possible for you to accommodate me here, while I wait for your husband's homecoming? The inns in the town are all full and there is not a bed to be had, neither for love nor money. My horse and I would be quite happy to share the same quarters, though not the same food — nor even the same drink, for he has no taste for wine,' he said, smiling.

Normally the merchants and traders who came to transact with the nobleman slept in taverns in the town; and if these lodging houses were full they took accommodation in private homes. She should have told the stranger so, but she was attracted by his good looks, his familiarity, his brusqueness and the way his eyes moved across her face and body, without censure, appraising it. She liked his unusual style of dress too, a velvet jerkin and red leggings, a knee-length cape subtly coloured in cinnamon (a daring shift from the more commonly worn ankle-length capes). He had a manner quite different from that of the emissaries and merchants who called on her husband.

Though Theodora knew her husband would not approve her giving lodging to an unknown person who offered neither letter of introduction nor identity papers, she agreed to accommodate the charming jeweller. 'You are welcome to stay here while you await my husband's return,' she said, escorting him out of the door and pointing beyond the courtyard and gardens. 'The stables are just across to the left beyond that walkway through the trees. You may lead your horse there while your room is made ready. I will have fresh garments put out for you and food prepared.'

'Thank you, I am most grateful,' he said, and bowed slightly. She watched him stride out through the heavily blossomed, overhanging trees, leading his horse. He looked down at the small fallen-star-shaped mauve flowers which carpeted the cobbles, and breathed deeply of their heady fragrance.

Theodora instructed Halla to put in order one of the more opulent guest suites, one seldom opened. She told her to dust it, prepare the bed with fresh curtains and linen, fill the vases with flowers, remove the coverings from the paintings and mirrors, and to fill a basin with warm fragrant water, that the visitor might wash.

Later, Halla carried his small travelling bag for him, and he thanked her courteously before closing the door. Frederic Montague stood at the open lead-paned window and looked down at the fields and orchards neatly laid out around the castle. He gazed out at the wide expanse before him, where the escarpment fell away, and saw in the far, far distance the line of the sea, for the day was crisp and the light clear and unimpeded. Then he sat on the four-poster bed, pulled off his boots and holed socks, undressed and washed. He put on the cream linen shirt and pantaloons, trimmed with maroon soutache braid, that had been laid out for him on the dressing stand.

Halla brought him a tray of refreshments — slices of turkey breast, shavings of smoked ham, quails' eggs and bread spread with rich butter; a carafe of newly fermented wine; a slice of fig cake. She took his clothes away to be cleaned, his boots to be waxed, and gave him a pair of soft leather slippers. In the stable his horse was brushed down and fed. Later it would be blanketed for the night.

The visitor remained in his room through the afternoon, resting; the nobleman's wife called for roses and magnolias to be picked, and for the urns in the hallway outside his room to be filled. Then she asked Halla to bathe and massage her and to nourish her hair with herb tisanes.

'Donna Theodora, we do not know this man,' cautioned Halla as she poured warm oil into her palms and began working it into her mistress's back. 'Should we not accommodate him with the labourers, or in the stables with the groom?'

'But he has introduced himself. He is a gentleman, Halla. A jeweller. How can we put him to sleep in the stable? He has business to do with my husband. It would be discourteous to send him off, tired and fatigued as he is. You heard him say there is nowhere for him to stay in the town. Don't concern yourself unnecessarily. The master will be well pleased that I welcomed this person and made him comfortable.'

★ ★ ★

That night Theodora invited her visitor to eat with her in the dining hall. She sat in her husband's chair and the jeweller sat in hers. They were served a meal of roast meats and vegetables, leek flan, cheese and fruit. The doors that led to the garden were wide open and the air of the night wafted in, heavy with the scent of flowers. An old wine was uncorked. The room danced in the candle-light. Theodora took pleasure in his presence, noting how handsomely the linen suit covered his strong body, glimpsing his chest, for he had not closed the upper buttons. She listened, enthralled, to his descriptions of certain plays and dramas that he said he enjoyed watching and was enchanted by the depictions of those playwrights and poets whose works he admired.

'I much prefer the works of the Italian writers above all others,' he said, leaning back, looking down into his wine and then at her. 'They have a passionate way with words. They capture so much of love and lust; so

90

much of beauty. But I must say, I have recently come across some central African poetry, translated and written from the original oral, for of course these black tribes have no written literature. That work is equally evocative and tantalizing. In fact it is quite blatantly erotic. I wondered when I first read it whether it was so sensual, so real to the senses, precisely because it had never been written down in its original composition, and was therefore never restrained in expression.

'You must know Solomon's Song of Songs? Well, it is reminiscent of that masterpiece in the way it likens the lover's body to natural non-human forms. It likens the woman's body to that of a leopard, and also to a civet. The hair of the beloved is said to be the coat of a lynx, her movement that of a serpent, lithe and easy, her dark skin the soft bark of some exotic tree, her lips the petals of swamp lilies. The very act of love-making, of penetration, is described as the arrival of rain after drought.

'Forgive me if I seem to lack decorum by describing this explicit poetry to you, but I just want to share with you its beauty and to show how the work leaves the reader reeling with a heightened sense of desire without being in any way vulgar. On the contrary, it is light and respectful of the human body and the art of love-making. It is really quite wondrous, and makes our own lovers, our poet-lovers, that is, appear rather limited,' he said, drinking from his wine, topping up his glass, sitting straight now and holding her eyes so that her cheeks flushed and she felt herself overcome with an unfamiliar exhilaration. She harnessed her composure, trying not to let her blush show, though aware that he saw it as his glance meandered around her face in the short silence while he waited for her response.

Theodora sipped from her goblet and said, 'I know little of poetry and literature. My husband's library is dedicated to travel and the natural sciences. But I would be pleased to read some of this work you mention, though I do know the Song of Songs, for there is a copy here. It is indeed beautiful. Perhaps you could give me the titles of these pieces you recommend and I will ask my husband to order them for me.'

'As a matter of fact, I have one here with me, which you are welcome to read. I copied it out just before leaving Siena and had it bound into a small folio. The ink was hardly dry when I left, for I could not bear to travel without it. This is one of a series of poems and it is about a doomed love affair. It tells of the love between an African queen and her slave. The queen is one of many wives, for African men are not bound to marry only one woman. They may have as many wives as they wish. And of course a king would have the choice of the most beautiful women of the land. This bride, the one in the poem, is clearly one of the younger wives, and certainly the most beautiful and his favourite.'

'Yes, I would like to read it. Thank you for your offer,' she replied.

'Some small parts are lost,' he said, 'but one can still get a sense of the whole, in the same way that one gets a sense of the whole form of Greek antiquities that have arms or legs broken from them. And there are a number of words which have not been translated from their African tongue. I surmise them to be the names of trees and birds. Even not knowing what they mean, they have a lovely sound to them, and do not detract from the beauty of the poem. On the contrary, they enhance it.'

'How did you come by this work?' she asked. 'Have you travelled into the central regions of Africa?'

'No, I am no explorer and no lover of dark unknown places. This work, and the others I speak of, came out of Africa with slaves. It was borne by them with all their lamentations. I cannot say how it crossed from their language into ours, but imagine the Arab traders saved these works from oblivion. Or perhaps a slave in high service, one who had become a scribe or an accountant, saw fit to record them. It's hard to say.'

When they had finished their meal, she invited him to walk along the turret and to view the expanse of the night sky. He carried the wine and their goblets, and she brought a brass bowl of candied ginger.

'We were speaking of written literature, of poetry and recited works. But wouldn't you agree that the star-filled sky is a form of narrative, one which is to be looked at, not read from a page, but one which is none the less evocative and marvellous?' she asked.

'The poetry of stars! What an extraordinary vision,' he said. A light breeze came up and played in her hair. As she walked up and down with him her silk gown whispered against her legs. They sat on a stone seat and he poured wine which they drank in silence. She thought she could hear bells ringing far off. He watched her strong profile as she sipped, then looked at the sky when she turned to face him. They could smell the sea in the night air.

Later, she escorted him to his room,

bidding him good-night. He drew a white rose from the urn outside his door, broke off the wet stem, placed the blossom in her palm and bowed courteously. Then he stepped backwards into his room and closed the door, bolting it quietly. Candles had been lit for him, the curtains of the poster bed drawn open, the sarsenet-lined crimson quilt pulled back, and a crystal carafe of port set with a goblet on his bedside table.

He took a pipe from his bag, filled it with aromatic tobacco and smoked, filling the room with the smell of aniseed while he drank directly from the decanter, finishing the port. He undressed, watched by a carved marble maiden which stood at the end of the room, seeming to smile approvingly at his muscular naked body. Then he blew out the candles one by one and eased himself between the fine, unbleached linen sheets of his bed.

Theodora had never before hosted a visitor on her own. She had never had the opportunity, either in the convent or here, to make overtures towards a friendship with someone close to her in age. Feelings of excitement rippled through her; she did not want to sleep, so stood at her balcony, holding the white rose, watching the night, looking out into the infinite distance, acutely aware of the stranger's presence in the castle, wanting to stay up with him until dawn, to talk until the sun came up.

Halla poured warm water into the stone tub and stirred sweet oils into it. She drew back the cover and prepared Theodora's bed.

'Mistress,' she again cautioned, 'I am afraid of this stranger's presence here, while the master is away.'

'Stop, Halla. Stop with your suspicions. It is not for you to make judgement on what I do. Now leave me, I want to be alone. I will put myself to bed tonight and bathe in the morning.'

★　★　★

The next day the nobleman's wife invited the jeweller to walk about the estate with her, which he was pleased to do. Whereas her husband was a gentle-featured man, with a smooth body and elegant stature, this man had a rude strength about him, which she found attractive. He had a closely cut beard, short-cropped chestnut hair, dark eyes and thick eyebrows. His broad, well-cared-for hands had tidily cut nails and wore no wedding band, but a signet ring of gold. He spoke eloquently, with a sharp turn of phrase, laughed easily and loudly without inhibition, teased her without thought to her noble position.

Donna Capelutto showed him her aviary, and he expressed awe at her collection of exotic birds. 'Sometimes, when my husband travels to forests and jungles, he brings me back a bird of fine plumage,' she said. 'They are brighter in the jungles and among their own trees. Their colours shine there and are more flamboyant. Here in my cage they long to be free, and their songs, though lovely to the ear, are different from those my husband hears them sing when they are at liberty.'

They strolled along the edge of the wheatfields and into the orchards; he picked a sprig of apple blossom and offered it to her; she tucked it into the lacing of her blouse.

'I wonder whether there are any poets among your slaves, whether one of them has heard the poem I spoke of,' he said as they watched the Nubians at work.

'They are not slaves,' she said. 'Though the older ones were sold into captivity as youths, and the younger ones were born into bondage, they are now paid free men, at liberty to go whenever they wish.'

'How is this?' he asked. 'Surely they have no value as free men?'

'They have been free for as long as my husband has been master of his lands. I know nothing of their value. Nor whether there are poets among them. But musicians there certainly are. They were quiet last night, for they worked till late in the barns, but listen tonight when you lie in bed: you will hear them play on their drums and flutes. You will hear them sing, too, but in their own language. I suppose that is where their poems lie, hidden in songs.'

Theodora led him to the apiary and the beekeeper took them through the dark cool vaults where honey was stored, opening one of the jars, letting them dip into the deep gold sweetness and taste of it. The beekeeper drew mead from a vat and offered them each a glass. They sat beside the fishpond, watching gold movements in the water and beneath gently floating lily leaves.

She sent the gardener to the kitchen to ask for refreshments, and the cook brought a basket of meats and bread and dried peaches with a flagon of mulberry wine. Donna Capelutto and her visitor ate their light meal in the pagoda of the herb garden while butterflies and bees went about their summer business.

'I know the whole world, though I have never myself travelled,' she said, 'for I help my husband with his maps. He has trained me in the art of map-making. We are in fact both cartographers to the Queen. I can, just from looking at the drawn representation of mountains and valleys, imagine them at their true height and exact depth. I am able to conjure up the breadth and force of rivers, merely from their depiction on a page. And, even without having seen the canyons and plateaux which my husband describes for me, I can visualize them from his notes, and then render them into a map that will be understood by any traveller.

'I also know where begin and end the silk route, the ivory route, the spice route, the slave route. I know all the markets of the world and where to buy silks and dyes and cottons and spun gold. I know the way through certain forests so thick as to be almost impassable; and at which point to traverse rivers so wide and wild that no ferryman dare cross.'

'St Petersburg is the furthest I have been, so I have no knowledge to compare with yours,' he responded, affecting a scholarly air, and they laughed.

'I should have liked to become an actor,' he told her. 'But my father was against this. Had I not followed him into the business of jewels, I would certainly have joined a company of players, and toured the country performing dramas and light verse. But there is not much income to be had as a travelling actor, for one depends on the coins thrown into one's hat. For me to have become an actor would have meant to break my father's heart, but also to be poor.'

'I have never watched play-actors,' she confessed, 'though there is a ruined Roman amphitheatre just beyond our lands.'

'Have you not? Perhaps your husband might invite one along one day, or even a group, to perform especially for you, the more so if you have a Roman theatre nearby.'

'Perhaps,' she said.

'The better actors,' he continued, 'can assume a character so realistically and with such conviction that you, in the audience, are completely taken in by them and the part they play. Why, you might even fall in love with one. It can be a shock to see such an actor, after a performance, attired in the garment and mode of his own personality. You might find yourself seeking out the character, the fictitious person, and not finding him. You then have to force yourself to realize he exists not, that there really is no life to him, no substance, no truth, except in the drama, which ends once he walks off stage and the curtain is drawn. All emotional contact ends once that curtain closes, even though there will have been much feeling between audience and actor during the play.'

He broke bread and placed slices of cold beef and caramelized onion on it, handing it to her, then poured more wine and said, 'Shall I fetch the African poem for you? We can read it together. It is a duet for two voices.'

★ ★ ★

'*My Lord*,' Theodora read aloud, as they sat in the enclosed white garden, where she had led her visitor after they had eaten, and which was heavily perfumed by blooming roses and jasmine, and where the marble nymphs of the fountain spouted water at each other.

> '*How is the face of love?*
> *Is it even-tide, when day descends*
>   *behind the mountain range*
> *leaving behind a frame of fire against the*
>   *peaks,*
> *or is it the sun itself, great ball of ochre*
>   *slowly moving down*
> *towards an unknown unnamed place?*
>
> *Is the face of love the night-black*
>   *darkness*
> *which hangs in curtained splendour,*

pierced through with shining stars?
Is it moonlight dancing in the shim-
mered forest leaves where fruit bats fly
and swoop?

Could the face of love be dawn
which lights each day?
Is it the iridescence of a wave's plume
borne in to the lake's edge
and carrying with it silvered fish and
terrapins
which shine in the morning radiance?'

'Enchantress,' he replied from memory, his
eyes closed, his voice deep and evocative.

'The face of love is here before me now,
and it is yours.
It is your skin — smooth red-brown bark
of mahogany;
it is your eyes — black portent seeds of
ebony;
it is your lips, open and full as a swamp
lily,
exuding rich fragrance, calling butterflies
to sup.

Love's face is your tongue, darting as a
jewelled lizard within your ivory
laugh;

it is the silver-pink blossom of mutsatsati,
the red flaming flower of mutiti; it is hot
    scarlet fire of aloes.
Love is not black night, not silver stars,
    not golden day at sunrise,
not patterned clouds; not moon. Let me
    reveal love's true design,

let me take your beaded wrap and cast it
    down;
then gaze upon your breasts, beige-
    brown as anthills,
and run my hands across your stomach
    rounded as the plains where lions
bask.
Let my tongue sip of you, urgently,
    as from a water-source soon to dry in
    drought.

He stood and strode out, as though on a
stage, addressing the eternally still face of the
marble water-nymph, imploring:

'Sing to me, beloved, sing to me your
    body's song of love,
and let me enter into you and row
    towards a place of dreams,
over silver lakes, and beyond, into that
    afterlife where no men walk,
but where abide only benevolent spirits

103

and the praise singers of beauty.

Within you I am no more mortal, but am
   a hawk winged and soaring,
I am one radiant, I am bolts of lightning,
I am rainstorm bursting
and pouring water into the drought-dry
   pools,
pouring goodness into the parched land,
filling the pools, the ponds, the cala-
   bashes with life.'

He turned to face Theodora, addressing
her as though she too were on stage, as
though she were the beloved listener:

'Drink now, drink, thou leopard, thou
   red civet,
drink of my waters, thou lover clothed in
   the copper coat of lynx.
Drink and become intoxicated, then hold
   me for ever,
thou lithe serpent winding about my
   limbs, my torso;
thou wondrous shining python — drink
   of me.

'Now, there is quite a bit missing here,' he
said, coming back to sit with her, his voice his
own again. 'But we know that their love is

forbidden. I told you last night — she is a queen and he a mere slave. They have managed to make love secretly. Some danger lurks. Perhaps they have been seen, or suspected. Whatever, he must leave and flee. Listen:

'Fair lover mine, how will we live again,
after this time of ecstasy is forced to end?
When the night has fled; when morning
  comes
and takes with it the cover and
  concealment of our touching,
we will be torn apart; our lips will be
  cruelly separated,
our embrace axed open
like a smashed baobab fruit; our seed
  scattered far and wasted;
the song in our hearts silenced by one
  strike of an assegai,
our flight of joy halted by sisal webbing,
our dance dragged to death in quick and
  choking sand pools.

'Now you recite; it is the Beloved speaking,' he said, and Theodora read from the folio:

'Sir, beloved sir! Let day come! I
  challenge it!
Let day tear apart the kaross of the night,

105

which hides our forbidden love.
Let day come! Let it find me naked at
your side, here among the golden
grasses.
My love is yours and yours alone.
What life is lived, if not with thee, here
among the proud muvonde?'

Neither spoke. Overhead, clouds banked up like great galleons upon an infinite and tranquil ocean. He took her hand and led her towards the fountain, where he turned to face her and drew her to himself. He held her softly so she could step back if she wished, but he had so dextrously woven an enchantment about her with his charisma and wit that she could not resist his body now taking over where the poetic left off.

He kissed her mouth, lightly at first, and then thrust his tongue in strongly (without the delicacy her husband employed, and in the broad light of day), forcing hers to dance with his. She tasted the slight bitterness of the tobacco he smoked each evening and the wine they had been drinking. She felt the resonance of a sigh, deep in his throat and chest, and was aroused by the weight of his desire as he pressed his body against hers. They stumbled backward into a tangle of shrubbery and jasmine and he began deftly, but without hurry, to undo the ties of her taupe satin blouse. Holding her shoulders, he ran his tongue across her breastbone and her whole body responded with a trembling of want. But here she stopped him. Though entwined and bound by the webs of his strong sexuality, she had sense enough to know it would be safer to embrace in her room, where no one could observe them.

★ ★ ★

Late that night, her visitor came to her. She was waiting for him, barefoot, dressed in a black silk kaftan, her body oiled and fragranced with ylang-ylang, her hair held back from her face with a rope of plaited velvet, a string of opals around her throat. She stood in the centre of the room, feeling her heart beating against her breast. He opened the door (without knocking), closed it quietly and bolted it behind him, strode up to her, took her in his arms, whispered at her ear, 'Madam, may I?' and kissed the base of her neck.

He did not extinguish the candles or the oil lamps, but left them to illuminate her room and cast shadows of their movements across the stone walls.

Unlike her husband, he undressed completely, revealing strong, sun-bronzed limbs, and a full male body, which she had never seen before, except in the paintings and frescoes that decorated the castle. He encouraged her to do the same, watching her as she discarded silk and velvet, exposing her pampered, marble-white skin to the warm light of the candles and lamps.

He held her close, then drew her down with him so they came upon their knees to the carpeted floor.

'My father was an angel,' she whispered, 'winged and robed in light.'

'Indeed? An angel? Well, my father was the Devil himself.'

'The Devil?'

'Aye, the Devil — God's bad angel. I am the Devil's boy. Thus I must warn you, madam, that I come with a history, so be wary of me,' he said. A warm wind blew at the curtains, billowing them like a sail into the room.

He kissed her shoulders and her ears, moving his hands across her trembling limbs, dancing his fingers lightly along her breasts. He bit her soft skin and played his hands over her stomach, under her arms, tarrying in the small of her back. Then he lifted her and carried her to her bed, where he lay upon her with the full weight of his firm body, and thrust into her, so she cried out as she felt herself tear and stretch to accommodate him. He left off, breathless for a moment, and then he resumed, puzzled, for he realized that he was the first man to have entered her. At the end, he poured a small circle of oil from the flagon at her bedside into his palm, then carefully massaged where he had gone into her, to soothe the newly wakened passageway.

They lay together, listening to the Nubians' songs rise into the night. 'There is sadness in them,' he observed. 'They must be songs of unrequited love. So I should not join in their chorus, as I lie here with you, who are so responsive to my charms,' he said, and laughed.

He remarked on the simple furnishings of her room, so different to those parts of the castle he had seen. Here were no statues, no paintings to decorate and enrich the space. The only embellishment came from the intricately patterned carpets on the floor and the fresco that adorned the ceiling. (A celestial explosion of cherubs and angels playing lyres and flutes, of birds and mythical creatures, all worked in a myriad of colours and finished with malachite-green and gold.)

'I was raised in a convent,' Theodora explained, 'with nothing in my room save a crucifix and my sleeping mat. I still enjoy that simplicity in my own quarters. I have grown used to the painted ceiling above me, though at first it overwhelmed me and filled my dreams with chaos. I would still prefer to sleep on a simple mat, but my Halla will not let me, though my husband understands this need, for he too prefers to sleep firmly, without a feather-bed.'

When the last of the candles and oil lamps fluttered out, and the first sound of dawn mentioned the close of night, he kissed her mouth, forcing it wide, biting the side of it, playing with her tongue.

He left off abruptly, pushing himself up from her, picking up his garments and boots, clutching them in front of himself to cover his nudity, then sashaying to the door with exaggerated movements, like a thief burdened with silverware. He affected a roguish smile, making her laugh, then went back to his own room, closing the door quietly just as Halla came up the stairs.

Donna Capelutto curled up on her side, wet from his kissing and their bodies' juices, run through with desire to be filled by him again and again, yet sure she was doing wrong, and thinking of her husband whom she loved but who was far away, and who had never ignited then quenched fire in her body as this visitor did.

'Halla, leave me to sleep a while longer,' she said as her servant drew open the curtains. 'Close them, and leave me to be alone.'

'Are you not well, mistress? May I bring you something to drink, a fragrant tea perhaps?'

'No. I want nothing; only to be alone a little while.'

When Halla left, hesitating at the door before closing it, her mistress stripped the undersheet from her bed, folded it up neatly and placed it at the bottom of her chest, underneath her clothes.

★ ★ ★

The visitor stayed with Theodora for nearly three weeks. By day the two strolled about the estate, enjoying the unfolding spring, drinking wines and fruit juices in the pagoda, nurturing their new love but always mindful not to touch openly, lest servants see them, sometimes creeping into the walled garden to kiss. By night, after they had dined, they closed themselves in her room and made love, listening to the night sounds of the estate in the background, to the music of the Nubians and the calls of her caged birds coming through her windows. Theodora would look up at the ceiling's garlanded angels and Cupids and feel enriched. The only time they were apart was when her lover left her early in the morning to escape Halla observing him in her mistress's bed; or when her servant bathed and dressed her.

Theodora asked Halla to pumice her body of all hair, so she was smooth and girl-like, and requested her more beautiful garments to be brought out for her; chose the beaded and embroidered above the plainer, simpler, everyday dresses; selected those coloured with the deep and rich dyes her husband had brought from exotic cultures. Her lover had never before seen fabric the colour of the setting sun, or cloth blue as a peacock's tail, or textiles the auburn of nutmeg. He had never before held in his arms a woman clothed in fabric with the feel of a butterfly wing. He undid for the first time buttons carved from ivory; unlaced dresses made from material threaded through with gold; kissed breasts covered in yellow silk.

At night, for their evening meals, Theodora ordered all the sconces and candelabra filled and lit, so the dining hall was extravagant with light. The jeweller asked to change places with her, to sit in her husband's chair, so that he could look both upon her and at her picture hanging behind her.

Once, he commented on the rubies painted around her portrait's neck, and asked her to wear them for him while he was with her. She called Halla to fetch the chain of rubies from her casket of jewels, and gave it to her visitor, who wound it about her neck five times. Their red colour, evoked by the candlelight, shone with a deep, resonant brilliance. He lifted her face and kissed her chin, and let his eyelashes trace across her mouth. He ran his hands through her shoulder-length hair; then down her throat; and across the crêped silk blouse which covered her breasts, hard with desire.

'Come upstairs, my angel's child,' he whispered hoarsely. 'I tire of seeing you wrapped in cloth. Come and undress for the Devil's boy.'

They left the dining room; left the dessert of flambéd apricots and pitted dates; took their wine and went upstairs to her room where each urgently undressed the other. Downstairs Halla, increasingly unsettled by the stranger's presence, unsure of her mistress's judgement, cleared the table while the portraits looked down sternly from their frames.

'This candlelight is a bewitchment, Donna Capelutto,' her lover said, casting her dress to one side. 'See how the blood of your rubies

113

dances against your waxen skin, entangling and enchanting me?' He kissed her brow, her lips, the rubies. He slid down to his knees as she stood before him, running his hands down her sides, and the tip of his tongue all the way from her sternum down her body, until he was kneeling. He kissed her inner thighs, parting her legs, biting her softly. Her flesh, which had been oiled and massaged up to three times a day for the past many years, was like that of a child, soft and unspoilt. He pulled her towards himself and lay on the carpet, drawing her to lie upon him, smiling up at the painted angels who watched from the ceiling as her body enclosed his and he entered her. The smell of lilies and jasmine laced the air.

Later, when they lay on their side, sated and wet with love, he stroked the nape of her neck and asked, 'How is it that your hair is kept so short, in so boyish a style? Does your husband not want it long and tumbling down your back? Does he enjoy this cut of a pageboy?'

'It is as the holy sisters always kept it; I am not used to long hair,' said Theodora. 'My Halla cuts it for me, and throws the pieces out for the birds to use in nesting. No, my husband does not mind my short hair. It is he who wears his hair long and plaited, in Mongolian fashion.'

★ ★ ★

One night Theodora led her visitor on to her balcony, where they sat under the sky's star-glittered velvet canopy. Earlier she had wrapped him in one of her Chinese gowns, and they had laughed because it was too short for him and did not reach to his strong, hairy calves.

He had unpacked her chests, admiring her clothes, holding them at arm's length or against her and even against himself. He found the hidden, folded bedsheet and pressed it to his face, breathing in its fragrance of love. 'May I have this?' he asked. 'To remind me always of our first night together?'

'Yes,' she said, smiling coquettishly. 'You may, though I thought to keep it myself.'

'Well, I think I deserve to have it. Now, let me clothe you, madam,' he said and drew from the pile of garments a simple indigo dress which he helped her put on, lacing and tying the bodice as he carefully positioned her breasts. She handed him a chain of gold bearing a single diamond and he fastened it around her neck, saying, 'I would like to take the place of your black woman-servant so as to attire you myself each day. Does she select what you wear? I fancy you have enough here to fill the costume box of a whole company of actors.'

'Halla? Sometimes she chooses for me. She enjoys matching jewels with fabrics. I think it is a bit of a game for her, and it gives her pleasure. She is well past working age, and my husband has had a cottage built for her close to the vineyards, where he would like her to retire in comfort, but she does not want to be away from us. She has her own quarters near the kitchen, so she attends to me faithfully day and night, and seems in fact to have forgotten that she once served my husband. She is quite devoted to me. I can do no wrong in her eyes.'

'And a good thing too, madam. For she might alarm your husband on his return with tales of your mischief, might she not?'

'Oh no, that Halla would never do. She pays no heed, really, to how I fill my day. She looks only to my comfort. Anyway, I am free to do as I wish.'

'How is that?'

'It is just so,' she said, and pulled the Chinese gown down from his shoulders, casting it aside and placing her lips upon his chest, softly, like a feather's touch; then spreading her hands across his broad hard breast muscles. He responded with equal tenderness, placing his mouth upon hers lightly, like a flake of snow, then turned her round and held her back against his chest, running his hands down her sides, undoing the ties, pulling the dress down, turning her to face him again then leading her to the bed.

Now, after their love play, they sat drinking wine and eating dates stuffed with pine nuts, she once more in the indigo dress, he wrapped from the waist in one of her silk shawls. Innocently at ease in his company, delighting in being able to share in his friendship and giving no thought to caution, Theodora told him, with the whole panoply of stars spread before them, that the earth was not a motionless body around which tiny stars moved and glittered.

'Tell me what the earth is, then, if not a silver tray balanced on the hands of angels,' he asked.

'It has long been known that the earth is round. The sea voyagers have confirmed this, and so has my husband. The Queen and the Church have accepted that the earth is a globe, a mass of matter, which holds itself aloft in the sky. My husband has a model of the round earth, which spins within a cradle. He had it made by a carpenter. The globe is in four pieces which fit together within the frame. He painted the land masses and the oceans on them. It is quite beautiful.

'But I must tell you, there is more to the earth than just its roundness. The earth is not motionless. It moves with other bodies around the sun.'

'Are you jesting?'

'No, indeed not,' said Theodora. 'And there is something else to marvel at. Did you know that the sun is in fact a star? That we bask in the light of a star?'

'A star?'

'Yes. It is our own star. And all the stars we see, far off in the sky, are not tiny twinkling little lights as you imagine,' she said. 'Each star is a huge burning sun, and around each of them move bodies which are not stars, but globes like our earth, some with their own moons.'

She pointed out the visible planets, naming them, so that he marvelled at her knowledge of the heavens.

'Where did you acquire this anarchic information, my lovely?' he asked, idly running his fingers through her hair. 'It opposes what the Church teaches. Do you know you can be burnt at the stake for it? You are to believe that the earth is a fixed point in the turning heavens.'

'Yes, I know that. But I never speak of this to anyone. It is private knowledge held only by a few people and shared with my husband and me by our closest friend.'

'Someone in the town?' he asked.

'Oh no,' she replied, 'he could not live safely in the town, for he would be seized without doubt and executed. No, he is a foreigner, a Jew from Syria who lives in Egypt. All his writings are kept in the university in Alexandria. My husband is his patron. He is a mathematician and he has unravelled, with certain other scholars, the secrets of the universe. He has studied much with an Italian, one who has made an eyeglass with which to look at the stars. Will you believe me if I tell you that with this eyeglass you can look at the moon and see upon it mountains and valleys and craters? The face of the moon is not perfect — it has not the smooth surface of glass it appears to have when we observe it with just our eyes. But there is something more wonderful in the night sky. If you look with the eyeglass, far beyond our moon, you will see four other moons which circle the planet Jupiter.'

'Have you gazed through the eyeglass?' he

asked. 'Have you seen these moons which such mere mortals as I cannot see with our naked eyes?'

'I have, yes. I have seen the wondrous moons,' replied Theodora. 'They are like pearls, round and white and luminous, and they move around Jupiter as though in attendance, like courtiers, or like dancers, with perfect time and poise. They are so beautiful that as you watch them you imagine that you hear some wondrous music playing — viola or cello or harpsichord. Yet you hear nothing, for they move in silence.

'But tell no one of this,' she cautioned.

'I assure you that I will tell no one these secrets you have shared with me. And I will never let it be known that I have held in my arms a stargazer; nor that I have made love to one who counts more moons in the sky than I. My lips are well and truly sealed,' he said, with a dramatic flourish of his palm against his mouth, his eyes glowing with mirth. He took her shoulders and turned her to face him, saying, 'And I'll only open them again if you kiss me.'

Above them, the quarter-moon hung in the night sky.

★ ★ ★

A refreshing sense of liberation and self-discovery, of completion, now flowed through Donna Capelutto. She realized for the first time how enclosed and limited her life as the convent-reared wife of a nobleman was. She reflected that she was but a passive partner in a marriage shaped entirely by her husband's life.

Seeing herself through the eyes of another, she saw an image both beautiful and enchanting. She could now call on all her knowledge of the earth and of the heavens, and share it with one who was not her teacher but a new, avid listener. More than this, she felt herself to be a true traveller at last, one who had chosen to take a journey into the unknown and in so doing had discovered her body and its pleasuring. A sense of daring overcame her. She had become an adventurer. I am a bird set free, she thought to herself, with my own wings and my own song. I am not caged.

Now, sitting at her lover's side, she took his face in her hands and said, 'When I think of the song of love, in the poem, I realize that I have never before heard or felt my own body's song of love. I have known nothing of it except what you have shown me in these past weeks.'

'Ah, that is because I am a master of love,

which very few men are,' he said gravely. 'Not many men know what to do with a woman's body; they know only how to satisfy themselves. Though I hazard to say that those black men in your husband's fields might know a thing or two.

'Now, shall I teach you something more, my dear apprentice? We have merely touched the surface, there is so much, so much,' he murmured at her ear as his hands worked gently to arouse her.

'Yes,' she whispered. 'Teach me more.'

'Right, madam,' he said, suddenly changing his tone, deepening his voice, feigning pomposity, drawing away from her and off the bed, wrapping her shawl about his neck. 'Let us begin with a little lesson in the anatomy of the male body, shall we? Do you see this large member down here' (he pointed in an exaggerated way), 'this rampant member down below here?' He gave a deep cough. 'Shall we call him something? Give him a name? Stop laughing! Madam! I implore you, or the member will retreat, and we will have no more pleasure! Do you wish to learn or not?'

'Yes,' she cried, laughing.

'What? What? What's that you say, madam, speak up,' he said, cupping his ear and squinting his eyes, and leaning heavily to one side, as though clutching a walking stick.

'Yes! Teach me! I beg you!'

'That's better! Right ho, then! Open up now, madam! Nice and wide, no coyness, please, dear noblewoman,' he said, and waddled across the room like an old retired medical doctor, prodding myopically at the air. 'But just show me which way to go then! Which way to get in!'

'Stop, or I will die laughing,' she implored.

He stopped joking abruptly, and came to lie with her, holding her against himself.

'You are a fine actor,' she whispered.

'That I am, madam,' he said.

'Your father should have let you pursue your wish.'

'So he should have. But then I would not have followed him into the trade of jewels, and I would not have met you. Indeed, I would not be here, waiting to do business with your husband, and instead doing business with your body. Speaking of which, Donna Theodora, what are we to do when your husband returns? I will not comfortably face him to place my order for black pearls. He will know, just from the way I look at you, that you are more mine than his. He will be entitled to call for a duel, and as I have come without a weapon he will lend me one of his, a lesser one, with some fault in its mechanism. My pistol will misfire and his bullet will burst my heart.

'We could of course, you and I, take poison when we hear his horse's hooves clatter against the cobbles of the courtyard, and let him find us dead and bound in each other's arms here on your bed. But that would be rather sad, and we would not readily make love after that. We will just have to ride away together; we could cross the sea for Sicily and settle there in an old villa.'

'I wish I could delay his return, though I love him,' said Theodora. 'Can you understand that? He is a good husband. I have everything I want. But now I want you, to keep to myself,' she said, smiling at him, lifting the folio and reciting from it:

'May time cease in its passage.
May the movement of the sun
halt in the wide sky, just before dawn,
    before the new life of new day.
May we remain eternally thus,
entwined and coupled by love; bound to
    granite by roots of munzvirwa.'

'Alas, the black pearls,' he said, and kissed her long and tenderly. 'They would have earned me such a fine sum. I too might have bought a castle.' Then he got up and poured more wine and they both drank, smiling across the rims of their goblets at each other.

Theodora ran her fingers across the poem's embossed cover and the gilt lettering of its title, *The Kiss*.

'Why does it have so simple a title,' she asked, 'when the poem is not about a single kiss, but about many and much more too?'

'Because of their last kiss, before he flees.'

Downstairs, in her own room adjoining the kitchen, Halla sat embroidering the collar of a shirt for her master, trying to still her confusion through the precision of her stitching. She was devoted to the nobleman. She had suckled him and his twin after their mother's death in childbirth, cared for them as they grew up, admired them through their adolescence and budding adulthood. When the young nobleman had returned home from one of his journeys horribly maimed, it was she who had oiled and massaged his scars, softening them. It was she who cared for him through his long lonely years of chosen solitude. It was she who had brushed his long hair before he married Theodora. But she also loved her young mistress, and her old mind did not want to have to contend with the confusion and fear which the visitor had forced upon her by enchanting the noblewoman with his worldly ways.

Halla was afraid of him and wanted him to go. She wanted her master to come back home. She did not know what to do or who to turn to for help, not daring to confide to the cook and other servants that their mistress had taken the stranger into her bed. Only that morning she had seen him come out of the nobleman's private quarters, but when she mentioned this to her mistress, Theodora had hushed her.

★ ★ ★

When Leonardo Capelutto returned home, when his wife heard the far-off sounds of his men and their horses, she did not call for Halla to hastily bathe and perfume her. Nor did she run out to meet him, as she always did. Instead she and the jeweller made love, hurriedly, like thieves of time stealing the last moments of life itself, drinking from each other like parched plants.

'Don't leave me,' she begged. 'Come back to me. Live in the town and watch for my husband's departure; come to me then, when he travels. He is away so often. I am alone for long periods. Then, we can live here as husband and wife, untroubled. And while you wait in the town, in those times he is home, you will want for nothing. I will send you

126

money, clothes, everything you need. And I will write to you every day and send you messages and gifts and tokens of my love. Only don't go from me; for I love you and will not know how to live without you.'

'Weep not, my beloved,' he said, wiping the tears from her face. 'I will not leave you. How can I go from you, who have captured my very heart and soul with your wondrous nature, like a net capturing songbirds? I too will want you day and night, hungering for you until the end of time. Nothing will prevent us being together, I swear this, not even your marriage contract. I will make some arrangement. Fear not. Leave it to me. Trust me, my precious one.'

They dressed and hurried to his room, where they packed his few things, and ran to the white garden. There, behind the fountain, with their shadow cast against the stones of the castle wall behind them, they said farewell. He rolled her bodice down so her pale breasts were exposed, kissing her there, and he bit her at the base of her neck, leaving a small mark, breathing in deeply the smell of her, to take it with him. Straightening her garment, he took his signet ring from his finger and gave it to her. Theodora unclasped her string of rubies and pressed it into the breast pocket of his jerkin.

He drew his cape about his shoulders and placed his cap upon his head, then bent once more to kiss her tenderly, holding her chin in one hand and the back of her neck in the other as she clung to his shoulders. 'Farewell, sweet mistress. I will never more smell jasmine without thinking of you, nor breathe in the fragrance of a rose without my heart aching,' he whispered, undoing her hold and turning from her. Then he strode purposefully to the stables, without haste so as not to draw attention to himself, and without looking back at her. He saddled his horse and mounted, bidding the groom goodbye and riding slowly out the back way as the nobleman and his riders reached the courtyard. Only then did he spur his horse and gallop towards the town.

Theodora ran to her balcony and watched him ride away, watched his cape billow in the wind and his form crouch forward over his steed to gain speed, watched the dust which the horse's hooves threw up behind him, watched until she could no longer see him. She drew closed the vermilion curtains, shutting out the afternoon sun. Then she lay on her bed, clutching the leather-bound poem her lover had given her, and wept bitterly.

Her husband strode into the hall and

called her name as he pulled his cloak from his shoulders and put down his weapons, puzzled that she had not come to meet him.

'Halla! Where is my dear lady?' he called.

'She sleeps, master.'

'Then wake her, good woman! Tell her I am back and longing for her. Tell her I ache to hold her; that I come laden with gifts; that I have missed her.'

He pulled off his boots, then climbed the stairs to his room, bolted it shut, undressed and bathed in the soothing oiled warm water which the servant had poured when she heard the horses enter the courtyard. He undid his plait and soaped his long hair, rinsing it, towelling it dry and rubbing oil into it. Then he dressed and sat out on the balcony of his room, watching darkness fall.

When he came in and lit the candles he noticed a folded cloth on his sleeping mat. He lifted it and opened it out. It was his wife's silk bedsheet, and it was marked by the dark stain of her virginal blood.

★ ★ ★

Donna Theodora Capelutto was sitting at her place in the dining hall when her husband came down. The table was spread with baked river fish and vegetables, fruits and mature cheeses, breads and a flagon of wine. He bent and kissed her hair, and she looked up at him as he touched her cheek. She closed her eyes, not wanting to tell him untruths or conceal anything from him, ready to tell him how she had loved a stranger, how she had given her body over to him, how she now cherished another.

Leonardo placed a finger on her lips, sealing them, not letting her confess. 'You made no vows, I remind you,' he whispered, so they spoke not of the man who had disturbed the private tranquil pattern of their lives, nor of what had happened in his absence. Instead he told her of his journey, and they ate and drank as they always did when he returned. He led her up to her room, where he extinguished the candles and oil lamps, undid his plait and lay with her so his hair fell heavily like silk about her, reclaiming her as his own. 'Theodora, my dear, my beautiful wife, what happened matters not. For I love you, nothing can change that,' he whispered, and kissed her, arousing her, making love to her his way, without penetrating her, clothed in embroidered pantaloons, in the dark.

But his wife's body had known more than this that he gave her, and now he could not appease the desires he stirred in her. This time her body was not satisfied. And he knew it. He wondered whether she had lain with one of the Nubians in the gardens or in the fields of barley; whether her white skin had been caressed by black hands. The Nubians gave off a strong animal energy, one he had himself often sensed. When they worked in the fields, humming to keep rhythm in their movements, half naked in the heat, they exuded a primal sexuality that might easily have caught and bound her. Perhaps one had dared to take her into his arms; perhaps she had succumbed. He tasted the salt tears that coursed unseen down her cheeks and said softly, 'Know always that I love you, whoever comes between us.'

When Leonardo left to go to his own quarters, Theodora lay naked on her side, curled up, holding her breasts, caressing herself and whispering to her lover's imagined presence. Her husband lay down and looked up at the painted ceiling, at the *putti* and Cupids and cherubs who would remain eternally innocent, untouched by the interventions of life, always garlanded and happy. Then he too curled to his side as sadness burdened him and his eyes filled with tears.

Halla, in her own room, relieved that her master was back and that the stranger had gone, sat on her bed staring at the floor. She could betray one or the other, or she need not betray either. Because she loved the nobleman and his wife equally, she chose to remain silent.

They would all three, the master, the mistress and the servant, behave towards one another as though nothing had happened to break the pristine, virginal world which the nobleman had so carefully created around himself.

★   ★   ★

The next day Leonardo Capelutto presented his wife with the notebook of this his most recent journey, into which he had pressed some grasses, and showed her the treasures his men had unpacked and laid out on the table and carpet of the downstairs room — pouches of opal and aquamarine; the rolled pelts of white wolves and mink; strings of green amber and rare white amber; a pouch of jewels coloured deep purple upon ultramarine; beautiful porcelain bowls; bronze statues and masks; a tusk of walrus ivory intricately carved with the images of mermaids and mermen.

He sent word to the merchants and traders' agents waiting in the town that he was back, and they came up to the castle to view and negotiate prices and buy. He apologized for the delay in his return — they had been waiting some weeks for him.

The merchants rode up to the castle each morning and spent the next few days assessing and selecting items and negotiating prices. Theodora walked among them, listening to them, watching them bale and prepare their treasures for transport. She hoped to see the jeweller among them, hoped to spirit him up to her room, where they could make love furiously while her husband busied himself with trade. She strolled in and out of the walled garden, hoping he would step out from behind the oleander and surprise her. She looked in the stables for his horse, but neither horse nor rider was there.

The noblewoman and her lover had not spoken about his life. Did he have a wife who bathed and oiled him, who rubbed and soothed his body, whose body he in turn caressed and fondled? she now wondered. And children? Had he filled his wife's body for her, once, twice, many times, with child?

But he belonged to her now, she knew this. Every part of her body had been mapped and claimed by him. He would come back to her, would leave what wife he had, forsake his children, of this she was certain. For how could he love another, now that he loved her?

Theodora asked the gardener to gather the flowers and leaves of foxglove, geranium, rose and juniper, so she might prepare a love potion to sprinkle into the wind. She asked Halla to again pumice the hair from her body; to oil her even at midday. She wore the same clothes she had worn when he was with her, seeking his presence in the fabrics he had caressed. She threaded his signet ring on to a gold chain and put it about her neck, tucking it into her clothes so it hung concealed at her navel.

She lamented not having cut a lock of his hair, or taken the pheasant feathers from his cap, or kept back his shirt, or his cape, anything that had once been wrapped around his body, and that she could now wear as an undergarment, or in bed when she dreamt of him. She searched his room for some small forgotten token, scoured the bed for one hair of his.

By the end of the week, all the merchants had conducted their business and gone, the viewing room was clear of its treasures and the nobleman's money chest full. Theodora's lover had not come back.

* * *

Three months would pass before the nobleman needed to travel again. In this time Theodora stayed always at his side. They worked together on a new map, and he described the route he had just journeyed and the problems he had encountered on his way home, by coming through a plague-quarantined area in Italy. But she was distracted. When he walked the lands, checked the orchards and the drying sheds, enquired about the crops or calves, she was with him. But her thoughts were elsewhere. If the sun beat down, if it was too hot, a Nubian would accompany them, holding a parasol above her to shelter her, sprinkling her lightly with rosewater. But Theodora's heart would burn with longing. When emissaries brought letters she looked through them, once, twice, three times, hoping to find one from her lover, before placing them on her husband's desk.

They ate three times a day in the dining hall; they drank pressed fruit juices mid-afternoon. At night she would undo his plait and brush his long hair, and she would imagine running her fingers through her lover's short beard, touching his lips, his ears. They would read to each other, though she concealed the African poem.

Late at night, when Leonardo slept, he

dreamt of desert sands shifting in the winds, of white bones bleached and scattered and lost. He would hear his twin calling him, and he would try to reach out to gather up the bones, but the wind would blow harder and his limbs would weaken and the pounding of his heart would wake him with a start.

One evening, over their meal, Leonardo confided his nightmares. 'I dream constantly of the red desert, the deserts of the red miners where I went in my youth, and where my twin was slaughtered. It is as though my twin calls me, wants to be fetched, made whole again. In my dreams the sands blow into my face, blinding me, so I cannot gather up the bones, cannot reclaim them. When I wake, I feel an urgency to go to the desert again, as though to a shrine, to pay homage, or to at least show my twin that I have not forgotten.'

He took a letter from his pocket, addressed by a goldsmith, someone from the western border regions whose name he was not familiar with, and continued, 'So it is indeed strange that I should receive this order and promissory note for red gold, which is so rare, and coloured like blood, and which can only be obtained in that very desert. Were it not for these dreams, I would not consider going, for I vowed never to return there. But I have decided to go.

'I will travel south, to reach the gold miners,' he said, looking across at Theodora, his elbow propped on the table, holding a glass of newly pressed wine and glancing through the crimson of it at a candle flame flickering to his left. 'I will trade with them at the edge of their territory, for they mine the interior, where no civilized men dare go.

'It will be a long journey — two months out from here and two months back — and I must leave soon, before the hot season, for then travelling will be impossible. I would like you to accompany me. I do not wish to leave you here alone without me. I am afraid to do so again. Will you prepare yourself, to take this journey with me?'

Donna Capelutto sipped her wine and said, 'But I am no traveller. I have made only one journey in my whole life. I am afraid to venture away from home, from the only world I know.'

'I will be with you, and my riders too,' said Leonardo. 'There is nothing to fear, only the unknown, but that becomes known as soon as you traverse it. We are too numerous to be attacked by bandits; and I know now how to deal with the red miners. You ride well, and we will not burden your horse with packs.'

'Will it be comfortable for me, this journey? What will I do without Halla?'

'It will be comfortable, yes,' he said. 'As was your travelling when I first brought you here. And beautiful. The desert has an austere splendour, quite unlike anything I have ever known. I should like to show you. I will fulfil Halla's role. I will care for you.'

What will he think, when he comes for me, if I am not here? she thought to herself. What will he do when he enters my room to find the curtains drawn about my bed, and me not lying there waiting?

Leonardo finished his wine and filled their goblets, saying, 'This will be my final journey, for I am weary of travel. My bones ache now from long times in the saddle. I will procure the red gold which has been ordered, and more of it, for it will bring me handsome payment. I will gather up what I can of the bone splinters my twin left in the sands. Then, my dearest, my career as traveller and entrepreneur will end, like a chapter of a novella. I will advise the Queen that I am too old now to travel, but that I will pay the stipend for a younger person to train and take my place as cartographer, someone from the Admiralty, some bright new cadet. I will stay at home then with you. Together we will read and walk the gardens, and watch the stars.'

Theodora looked down at the napkin on her lap, lifted it and wiped her lips. There is another in my life now, she wanted to say. Though I love you as a husband, this other I love as I have never loved before. This other I love with my whole soul. This other has done something to my body so that I burn inside wanting him. He will be searching for me among the lilies, in the white garden, down at the apiary, not finding me, thinking I have gone from him, if I come with you.

She lowered her eyes and ran a hand across her belly. There was silence between them. Leonardo looked up at the painting of his wife, then down at her. He thought to ask her to replace the diamonds that now adorned her neck with her length of rubies, for he loved their crimson colour which sat so well on her albumen skin, but he did not.

Instead he said, 'I feel so afraid, suddenly. I am afraid to lose you. I asked for no vows so you could be free. Now I fear something deep. Do not turn away from me. I am nothing without you. Come with me. Travel this last route with me.'

'Do not be afraid,' she said, not wanting to face this new vulnerable side of him, yet noting how weary he looked. 'I will travel with you. I will never leave you alone.'

★ ★ ★

There was to be another visitor, and he would arrive shortly before Leonardo and Theodora set off on their journey together. After the years of seclusion, a second man arrived at the castle to alter the tempo of its monastic tranquillity. This caller was the nobleman's cousin, the Inquisitor, the Queen's confessor, and he came, uninvited and unexpected, by horse-drawn carriage, with a monk in attendance, requesting lodging for one night, just as the sun had gone down and darkness was settling. The house servants averted their eyes and bowed their heads when he walked in.

Leonardo was both surprised and angry to see him. 'You are not welcome here. How dare you presume to enter my property? What do you want?' he challenged.

'I am travelling in this region, and find myself caught between day and darkness,' replied the Inquisitor. 'I will not get back to the abbey now without encountering bandits and have no choice but to stop here. I ask only one night's accommodation. Surely you will not deny a fellow Christian this, and one who is your cousin at that?' he said.

'It is foolish to be travelling at this hour,' said Leonardo, 'and I object to your play on my sympathies, this presumption you have that I would not do something so cruel as send you on your way. You are no friend of mine, and I am not pleased to have you as a blood relative. I feel no compassion for you; you deserve none. So my welcome is false, and I will permit you to stay only because I am not a heartless beast. But you must be gone by early morning. And I warn you not to flaunt yourself or take advantage of my hospitality.'

The Dominican was shown to his room, and his companion to the servants' quarters. Warm water, towels and scented soap were brought to him and, later, trays of bread, meats, cheese and wine, so that he might eat alone and refresh himself.

That night, the nobleman and the Dominican were already seated at the table when Theodora came down to dine. Halla had dressed her in a plain robe and placed about her neck a simple gold chain and cross, saying softly, as though the very walls were listening: 'He is a cruel man. He hates the master and is jealous of him. You must say nothing to him.'

Her husband stood when she entered the dining hall and introduced her to the Inquisitor, who did not rise from his chair but held out his hand so she might kiss his ring. Had Halla not cautioned her, she would have known instinctively to say nothing.

Over their meal, the Inquisitor sat back and said, 'It is many years since I last set eyes on you, dear cousin. We last spoke at the reading of your father's will, if I recall. And you hardly gave me the time of day, instead working in that walled garden with your back to me the whole day. Or am I mistaken, have we spoken since?'

'You are correct. That was the last time we spoke directly, face to face. And though you don't lighten my heart with your presence now, I must ask what you are doing out here in the country, so far from your comforts. Why were you still on the road at dusk? Surely you know that by mid-afternoon you should already have stopped at a lodging house. Your jewelled cross and ring would be fine loot for a highwayman. He need work no more after relieving you of them.'

'My attendant monk made some errors,' said the Inquisitor. 'He took wrong turns, bringing us here to your threshold instead of to some more suitable and welcoming lodging. But as it is, Her Highness, knowing I would be in the area, suggested I call on you and personally convey her warm regards to both you and Donna Capelutto. Thus I judged it high time I met your wife myself. In fact I was wondering whether there have been any baptisms in the Capelutto family, though I have not had news of any childbirths blessing you.'

'The Queen Marie-Ursula would never send you here. Don't hide your own intentions behind her name,' said Leonardo.

The Inquisitor did not respond. Instead he said, 'Madam, I was not invited to your wedding, or we would have met sooner; I merely heard about it when Her Highness mentioned it in passing. Were your husband a little more caring of your status, he might have brought you into society, to meet with ladies of the court and make some friends and, indeed, to meet Her Highness. For reasons known only to himself, he has chosen to keep you here in the wheatfields among peasants and slaves.'

The Inquisitor watched her pointedly for a while, until her husband replied, 'You well know that there have been no children born to us and therefore no baptisms. And you know too that there are no slaves on my estate.'

'Perhaps, Donna Capelutto,' replied the Inquisitor, 'the Lord will still deign to bless you with a child. I trust you pray and lead a Christian life.'

When Theodora did not respond, but instead looked down at her hands as she twisted the rings around her fingers, the Inquisitor turned back to her husband, who wore a look of steel across his face, saying, 'Don't overstep your mark, Diego. Mind what liberties you take with your tongue, or you might find yourself conversing with my sword.'

'Ah, listen to this boyish threat from my young cousin. Shall I take it seriously?' he challenged. 'I trust that was a slip of yours, addressing me by my baptismal name. Or must I remind you of my ecclesiastical title?

'To tell the truth,' he continued, returning to their earlier conversation, 'I did travel to this region some years ago. I came to deal with an outbreak of satanic practice; in fact I recall sending you word of this. Have you forgotten?'

'I do remember, yes,' answered Leonardo. 'And I remember the smell of burnt flesh which lingered in the air for weeks after you had left.'

'Ah. It lingered, did it? As a good reminder, then,' retorted the Inquisitor, pushing his glass towards his cousin to be refilled.

'But, to continue, I must say that, had I come to these parts at other times, I would certainly have called on you, and hoped for

144

some warm welcome. We are cousins, after all. The near-same blood runs through our veins. As it is, I am here now on ecclesiastical business. I come to give notice to the local office of the Inquisition, housed, as you know, in the abbey, of a certain Jew from the Levant, a scholar of sorts, who has proclaimed he knows more of the heavens than does the Church itself. It is suspected that he is here somewhere, travelling in these parts. The office in Rome has alerted me to the fact that he carries with him an instrument of the Devil with which he views the stars, and then proclaims the heavenly lights to be something they are not. He insists, among many heresies and blasphemies, that the earth does not sit motionless, as placed by God, at the centre of the universe, but that it travels around the sun.

'We have cleared our own universities of such heathens, and burnt all their theses and propositions. But this Jew has a seat at a foreign university, one governed in coalition by heathens — Jews and Moors and the unbaptized. He has been tried *in absentia* and condemned to death by burning at the stake. Perhaps you know of him? Balthazar Ben Jehuda of Syria is his name.'

'If I knew him, cousin, would you require

that I surrender him into your hands?' asked the nobleman.

'Indeed. Yes. It would be wise and in your own interests to hand him over, for the sheltering of a heathen is in itself an offence punishable by death,' said the Inquisitor, flicking a finger against his still-empty goblet so its crystal chime rang through the air.

'Let me hope, then, never knowingly to harbour such a person,' said Leonardo, walking round the table, refilling their wineglasses and laying a reassuring hand on his wife's shoulder as he passed behind her chair.

'Let us hope so,' replied his cousin, raising his glass. 'I have much to do at the abbey so will leave early in the morning. But let me say that it has been a pleasure being in our family's ancestral home again, and a pleasure to meet your wife.'

He drank the last of his wine, then said, 'Tomorrow I would like to say Mass in your chapel, before I leave. I trust you will both be there to receive the holy sacrament, and all your servants too, including your black men, whom I feel compelled to baptize and whose pagan music has been resonating since my arrival here, causing me great concern. You should put a stop to their demonic drumming and chanting. It should have no place in a

Christian home. They are inviting more than the Devil to infiltrate, but all the Devil's entourage as well. You are allowing them to create a regular Hades here. You can be quite sure they are dancing too, and half naked without a doubt, working themselves into all manner of sexual frenzy.'

'We will decline your offer to say Mass,' said the nobleman, remaining seated. 'Brother Matteo calls each Sunday to offer it. The sacraments are celebrated regularly and confessions are heard. My Nubians are all Christian. There are no pagan rituals performed on my lands.'

'You might be surprised. If they drum and dance for the Devil, they are likely to offer sacrifices too. I urge you to bring them into line. They are no better than Jews. You will find yourself or your wife with your throats slit and your bodies drained of blood, sooner or later.

'As far as not allowing me to celebrate Mass here is concerned, that is your wish and I cannot go against it. It is a pity, though, would you not say, to deny your wife and black men the chance to receive the holy eucharist from my hand?' said the Queen's confessor, pausing for a response. When none came, he said curtly, 'I will leave at nine in the morning. I will take breakfast in my room, if you'd care to have it sent up to me.

'Good-night, Donna Capelutto. The Lord bless and keep you. The Lord invest progeny in you, to give your life meaning.'

'I warn you, Diego,' said the nobleman, rising to his feet, pushing back his chair.

'Good-night,' said the Inquisitor, a thin smile slicing his face as he left the dining hall.

⋆   ⋆   ⋆

Leonardo and Theodora remained at the table until the last of the candles had burnt down. The atmosphere had been tangibly cut through with precision and cruelty. They went upstairs to Leonardo's quarters, where they sat together on the ottoman. She felt as though a sword had passed through her heart. Overwhelmed by all that had happened during the past weeks, and by her meeting with the Dominican, she turned and laid her head against her husband's shoulder, drawing breath through his sandalwood-scented plait; thinking of the ring she had been compelled to kiss and wiping her mouth on the hem of her robe. Reassuringly, her husband ran his fingers through her hair.

'He frightens me. He wants Balthazar. How does he know about him?' she asked solemnly.

'Yes, he is a fearsome man. And I too wonder how he came to know about Balthazar, but more so, how he came to know that Balthazar is travelling through these parts now, when I have only received news of this myself today.'

'But the autumnal equinox is months away. Why is Balthazar coming now?' she asked.

'He wrote to say that he came across an ancient Babylonian almanac which predicts a total lunar eclipse within the month. He is on his way to view it with us, and to verify the prediction. He has already left Alexandria. I sent an emissary this afternoon to try to apprehend him on the road, and urge him to go back.'

'But we are due to travel,' said Theodora. 'Should we not stay, and wait for him?'

'I cannot postpone this journey. It will be too hot in later months. I have the promissory note for the red gold. I must honour it.'

They were quiet for a long time, each with their own thoughts.

In the soft light of a single candle, Theodora saw sorrow in her husband's eyes. She stretched up and tenderly undid his plait, pulling his hair down on to his shoulders, then took him by the hand, blew out the light and led him to his sleeping mat, where she took off his blouson before undressing herself, in the dark.

Throughout the night and into the dawn, the steady beating sound of a single drum permeated the air, enfolding the property, protecting it, it seemed, from harm.

★   ★   ★

The next evening, the nobleman paced the dining hall, looking down at the symmetry of the mosaic floor, comparing its order to the now broken ranks within his own life. For years he had kept everything predictable and to form. Now a new energy had entered his life — a zephyr, a dust devil — and it had torn at the tranquillity he had created around himself and his wife.

Theodora entered the dining hall, disturbing his reverie. He took her in his arms, then led her to sit at the table, where they sat in silence while Halla served their food.

'I have received word,' said Leonardo, 'that the Pope in Rome is intensifying his persecution of scholars, and bringing those who hold any scientific view not condoned by the Church before tribunals.

'Balthazar's Italian friend, Galileo, has attracted enmity and suspicion for treading on holy ground. He has been detained and placed under house-arrest in Rome. Under threat of torture and death he has renounced his view of the universe and declared his own scientific writings blasphemous. For his own safety he has turned his attention to the less perilous pursuits of poetry and literary criticism.

'My concern for Balthazar has deepened. Until now he was safe visiting us, as a foreign citizen. My cousin would not have dared risk diplomatic scandal by apprehending him. But from now on we must caution Balthazar to remain in Egypt and not enter Christian territories. We will visit him at his home in future.'

They finished their meal in silence, then went out to sit in the garden.

The next day they began preparations for travel. This was to be her second journey.

★　★　★

Cardinal Uriel of Catalonia was baptized Diego Capelutto Loyola. His mother was the sister of Jasper Capelutto. She had married into the Loyola family, taking with her a large dowry and spending the first year of marriage enjoying the shallow life of court society. But she too, like Leonardo's mother, had died in childbirth. Uriel was brought up by a father who womanized and gambled, who lost his fortune and then put the young boy into the care of monks in a Catalonian abbey, meeting his own end in a duel.

So the cardinal's early life of seclusion was not unlike Theodora's, except that she was loved and taught about the beauty of prayer and inner life, while he learnt only the overt cruelty of monastic rigour, the arrogance of dogma and the strait-lacing of religion. He took early vows and worked a swift way up through the ecclesiastical ranks, professing a piety that veneered his ambition and a selfish, single-minded quest for power.

As a cardinal of noble birth, he was assigned to say Mass each morning at the palace and to hear the confessions of the King and his only child, Princess Marie-Ursula. The King died while the Princess was still grieving the loss of the Capelutto twins — the one, her lover, by rejection and the other by death. Too young to face this compounded anguish alone, and with the additional burden of becoming monarch, she turned for support and consolation, in the confessional booth, to the cardinal. He positioned himself at the centre of her grief, as a small black spider, then spun a web which was beautifully symmetrical, carefully taut and masterfully binding, drawing back the curtain of protocol which separated them and taking up the role of friend, companion and confidant.

Marie-Ursula hated every moment of the long, pompous coronation ceremony. Her head throbbed and her neck ached from the weight of the solid gold, jewelled crown, the heavy, ermine-lined cloak, and the load of all the gems sewn into the cloth of her gown. The cathedral was hot and stuffy, the long intoned prayers and liturgy seemed endless, the incense suffocating. That night she excused herself from the celebratory banquet and cried herself to sleep. The cardinal took it upon himself to represent the new Queen and dined in her place with the dignitaries. Ambassadors and important personages ate and drank from gold plates and goblets in her honour but without her presence.

Through the following few days, the cardinal comforted Marie-Ursula with prayer, read the Bible aloud and called a trio of musicians to play for her. She cried often and refused her food. One evening she told him that she did not want to be queen but to live in the Capelutto castle with Leonardo. Marie-Ursula told the Dominican of her devotion to the young nobleman, and the fact that they had once been lovers. 'I love him, Holiness, and I want to return to him — it does not matter that he is scarred; I love him still. He is so anguished, so alone. He will not let me comfort him, but wants to live apart, like a hermit. But I can heal him, I know I can, for we love each other so deeply. And once he is well, we will marry and be happy together.'

The cardinal called her into the confessional, to properly receive the sacrament. An intricately carved grille separated the solemn voice of the divine spokesperson from his distraught penitent. 'Did you indeed sin carnally, my child?' he asked.

'We did sin with our bodies, yes, Holiness. I confess that while we were unwed we touched each other's nakedness,' she said.

'Did you allow him to enter your body, my child, as a married man might enter into his wife's body?'

'Yes, Holiness.'

'Speak louder, my child. Speak clearly. Express your sin fully.'

'Yes, Holiness, I allowed him to enter my body as though we were husband and wife.'

'You allowed him to enter your body as though you were husband and wife bound together by holy matrimony in the eyes of God?'

'Yes, Holiness.'

'Repeat your sin fully, my child, and say his name.'

'I allowed Leonardo Capelutto to enter my body, as though we were husband and wife, bound together by holy matrimony in the eyes of God.'

'This is a grievous sin, my child. Only those bound by marriage can commit such acts, and then only to procreate, to fulfil God's command that we bear fruit and fill the earth. Did you commit this deed once? How often did you show him your nakedness? Did you do this by night or by day?'

'We committed this deed three times, Holiness. I showed him my nakedness. Once by day and twice by night.'

The confessor was silent for a while, then said, 'What other sins have you to confess, my child?'

'That is my only sin, Holiness,' she said.

'Do you still think of your seducer?'

'Yes, Holiness.'

'Do you still want after him?'

'I love him, Holiness.'

'This is not love, child. It is lust. Lust too is a grievous sin. There will be much penance for you to offer. You have tarnished your soul and your body.'

'I will offer whatever penance you give me, Holiness. For my sins.'

'I must pray for guidance, child, to know what measure of penance to give you. I do not absolve you now of your sin, but tell you only to reflect on the depth of this depravity.'

The confessor left the booth and escorted the crying Queen to her bedchamber. He closed the door of her room, locking it. Then he sat in her ante-room, where he was brought wine and a dinner of suckling pig and eggs served on a silver plate.

The next day the cardinal called her to confession again. From behind the grille he said, 'My child, I am compelled by divine inspiration to grant you forgiveness without penance. Instead of offering penance, you are to reflect upon your divine-given responsibility as monarch. Your duty, that which God wishes of you, will be revealed to us in time.'

Despite the pressure the cardinal placed on her in the confessional, the young Queen wrote to the nobleman each afternoon, sitting at her window. She signed and sealed her letters, kissing them before handing them to her confessor to dispatch. He in turn burnt them each evening once she was asleep.

'Holiness, why does he not reply? I merely write words of comfort and friendship. I demand nothing,' she asked.

'It is because he is a mere seducer; one who cunningly seeks after his own interests and comforts; one who has forfeited his soul to the Devil's cause. Need I remind you that he tore your maidenhead? That he stole your virgin purity? Highness, discard him; cleanse yourself of thoughts about him. I recommend that you stop writing to him. Let us spend those hours you devote to your correspondence by walking through the palace gardens. You can take the fresh air and I will recite the rosary as we walk.' (Capelutto is but a ruined carcass, the confessor thought to himself, worth no more than a bull's hide.) 'You are to forget Capelutto, for he is a sinner. It was he who led you to commit these despicable, carnal deeds. You are to stop thinking about him and face forward.'

So she stopped writing to her beloved. But she could not stop herself loving him. In her heart she would whisper his name, and tell him that she loved him still, invite him to return to her.

When she strolled with the cardinal through the rose gardens, or when she sat with him at the fishponds in which orange carp darted, she asked many questions on the nature of God. 'Why has God punished me by removing, in one blow, everyone I love — my betrothed, his twin, and my own father, the King? What did I wrong? Even at birth He saw fit to strike me, by shrivelling this leg. Could that not have been enough?'

'The ways of the divine may seem mysterious. God may appear to give a free hand to suffering, allowing it to strike and strike again. But there is a pattern and a purpose; there is always reason in all God's doings. Though you may not see it because of your innocence, I see it clearly. The divine wants of you a focused life, a life untrammelled by affairs of the body and heart. The divine wants you to be a good Christian ruler, singular and devoted to His service. His mission will be made clear. In the meanwhile, accept that He wants you unwed, celibate and pure. And let us celebrate that He has placed me here, to guide and succour you. I am at your side day and night, my dear. I will leave all my other work and assign myself to you until you are strong. I replace betrothed, friend and father. You have nothing to fear.'

She had turned to embrace him, to shelter in his mature arms, seeking paternal comfort from him. But he had pushed her gently away, saying, 'No, Highness, we must never touch. Not even hands. I remind you that I am a servant of God. I am with you only in that role. I am your confessor, your friend, your faithful servant. But my body is God's, bound by my religious vows.'

The cardinal sent her ministers off, telling

them she was weak and frail and aggrieved. He ordered his bed to be set in her ante-chamber, and sent her handmaidens to sleep downstairs with the palace servants. He forbade her visitors, claiming he was protecting her through her period of prolonged mourning. Cardinal Uriel watched over every one of her moments, even those of sleep, for he gave to her each night a draught of laudanum, and would pace about her bed, looking at her as she slept, deeply drugged. Sometimes he pulled her bedlinens down, and the lace of her nightdress open, so he could look upon her white young breasts. Sometimes he placed his palms upon them. Sometimes he bent over her and kissed them. Sometimes he undressed and lay naked next to her, touching her. Once he dragged his nails down from her neck to her navel, drawing blood.

In the confessional she told him that she had fearful dreams, from which she could not wake, of travelling down to the Underworld garbed as Eurydice, watching Orpheus try to bring her from the bowels of hell, but would find herself tangled in the Devil's barbed tail, unable to follow.

'We used to play at Orpheus and Eurydice, Leonardo and I. I dream of those plays, but only now the dreams are demonic, as though the Devil himself is in my bedchamber, molesting me,' she said. 'Holiness, I cannot show you, for I cannot remove my garments before you,' she said, 'but I have terrible claw marks upon me, where the Devil touched me.'

'Pray with me, child. Do not weep. Hush. Pray with me for guidance. God will give me to understand clearly the message which He presents to you in your dreams. Let me meditate upon this, to understand more clearly the divine wish.'

A few days later, while they walked through the gardens, he said, 'I understand what it is God wants of you. In my hours of prayer He spoke directly to me. I heard the voice of God distinctly.

'The divine wishes you to clear from our country all the Devil's Judaic energy. You are to make me His instrument. If you permit me, I will work with the Office of the Inquisition in Rome to banish every last vestige of Judaism from our country, for Jews are the Devil's instruments. It is they who spread the ungodly notion that the sun is the centre of the sacred universe. It is they who poison the minds of scholars with demonic descriptions of stars being other than the lights of angels glorifying the divine. We must rid our land of them. Once they are gone from the farthest corners of our country, you will not dream this darkness again. The Devil will not touch your flesh another time. This I can promise you. Fear not, I am with you. I am at your side. I am your protector.'

★   ★   ★

The cardinal prepared documents, copies of which were sent to the Office of the Inquisition in Rome, naming himself as Chief Inquisitor of the kingdom and vesting himself with the unfettered power to define that which was heathen and blasphemous; to expel Jews, to confiscate their property and title, to put them to death by fire if necessary. The young Queen signed and sealed all the declarations.

Working methodically and with precision, and in collaboration with the Office in Rome, the cardinal unleashed an army of torturers and sadists who acted in the Queen's name, and in the name of God, right up until the day she died and a new age of enlightenment was ushered in. Synagogues were plundered and razed. Jewish scholars and physicians were stripped of their titles and forbidden to work at universities. Religious books, scientific treatises, scrolls and Talmudic teachings were seized and condemned in sham trials, then burnt in huge public fires. White ash rained for days, like snow. The cardinal decreed that any non-Jewish scholars who presented a view of the world and creation that contradicted the teachings of the Church would be judged guilty of blasphemy, a crime punishable by public burning at the stake.

Once the cardinal had established himself as Inquisitor, once his religious authority was secure and unassailable, he distanced himself somewhat from the Queen, visiting her only for confession and to administer the holy sacrament.

The cardinal himself took over a small abbey, which he named Royal Abbey, not far from the palace. He governed his community harshly. Though he himself enjoyed the comfort of a feather-bed and fine linen vestments, his monks were compelled to wear robes of the coarsest sackcloth. They ate no meat, only root vegetables and grains, and slept on thin mats on the hard floor. He dined and drank well in his own quarters, and satisfied his carnal lusts on country girls from the surrounding homesteads whom he threatened with damnation in the deepest depths of hell to secure their service and silence, enjoining them to creep through his private entrance at night.

★ ★ ★

As she grew and matured, and came to terms with her role as monarch, Queen Marie-Ursula was pleased to have some distance between herself and her confessor. Though she depended on him emotionally and spiritually, she was afraid of him, for he angered easily.

Her ministers trained her in secular affairs of state and nurtured in her a keen interest in governance. Foreign heads of state called on her and ambassadors presented their credentials. Her generals and admirals gave reports of the army and fleet. Neither she nor her ministers supported the cardinal's harsh treatment of Jews, for there were doctors and philosophers and economists among them. In her father's day, the Jews had financed the fleet, paying a dedicated tax for its construction and maintenance. But as she had signed all matters of state religion over to her confessor through the head office of the Inquisition in Rome, she could not easily rescind his powers. This would have involved a tribunal in which she would have had to defend the position of the Jews publicly. So she never confronted the cardinal or tried to temper the powers she had vested in him, and never properly understood the ruin he was

163

inflicting on her country's fabric of tolerance. Her ministers did not dare make public statements in support of Jews, for that would have been punishable by death.

One day, after a meeting with her statesmen, one of her ambassadors, recently returned from Egypt, presented her with a map rolled into a tube of vellum.

'Highness,' he said, 'while in Cairo I met an aged gentle Jew, and when he heard that I was soon to be home he asked me to deliver personally and into your hand only this *mappa orientalis*, which was apparently executed by one of your subjects, the nobleman Capelutto. You are aware that the Jews keep high positions in the libraries and universities of Egypt, so I came into contact with him in the course of my diplomatic work. I did not purposefully seek him out. But having conversed with him, I found him greatly knowledgeable. He asked me to convey to you that a map such as this is worth a great deal, not only in gold but in political power, and that there is demand among other monarchies for such, as all wish to achieve dominion over the world.'

The ambassador and the Queen's secretary unrolled the map and weighed its corners down. It was drawn in inks of various colours, depicting rivers, mountain ranges and plateaux, and showed the east coast of a continent with the ocean clearly marked. Passageways were highlighted by dotted lines, so too settlements. (A modern traveller would identify the east coast of China.) In the right-hand corner, the map was signed simply *Leonardo Capelutto*.

The Queen stood silently looking at the work, so artistically rendered, and placed her finger upon the signature. Then she turned to her ambassador, saying, 'I would like to know how the nobleman Capelutto came to have knowledge of these mysterious territories. Does he travel himself, or has he drawn from hearsay and the writings of explorers? I fear that if I write to ask him he will not reply. Will you kindly call upon him in person and ask him yourself, then bring me this information.'

The ambassador travelled to the Capelutto estate, and reported on his return that the nobleman was not at home, but that he was travelling through faraway terrains and would be away some months. 'He has become a voyager, explorer and map maker, Highness,' said the ambassador. 'His housekeeper told me that when home, he spends his solitary hours drawing maps.'

'Return to his castle and await his return. Then tell him that he is to travel for the Crown. He is to represent his queen on his journeys of exploration, and he is to map them for her, so that the design of the world belongs to her and her alone. His queen commissions him to be Royal Cartographer. He is to have no choice in the matter.'

⋆   ⋆   ⋆

'You will allow the Devil to enter, Highness, after all my pains to exorcise his malevolence,' warned her confessor sternly when she told him that she wanted the nobleman to be in her service. 'I have cautioned you to have no dealings with Capelutto,' he intoned. 'Did he not cause you to sin carnally? And if that was not enough, did he not break your heart once he had your virgin blood upon his loins? Highness, I warn you, he is a harbinger of evil. Your dreams will turn again. Satan will claw at your body and draw blood. I remind you of his nails, Highness; and his barbed tail; and his foul odour.'

'I implore you, Holiness,' said the Queen, 'to do your utmost to keep the Devil from me, for surely he will madden me should he enter my bedchamber again. Capelutto will not come to the palace, I assure you. He will not enter the palace grounds. He will merely depict his journeys so that I can build up a library of maps, which my army and fleet will use, and which will permit me to annex new territories as my own.

'I beg you, my beloved cardinal and confessor, to whom I owe my stability and strength, and for whose presence I thank God every day, not to be angry with me. But permit me to say that my ministers have counselled me well in matters of state and economy. If unknown territories are not marked as mine, other kings will take them. Capelutto's maps will serve me well.

'Come, pray with me, Holiness. Bless me,' she said, kneeling before him, taking out her rosary and closing her eyes. As he raised his hands to bless her, trembling in anger, he realized that he had made an error, allowing her to govern with her ministers. He should have kept closer watch over her, tighter control. The ministers should have been dismissed, and he alone ruled alongside her as spiritual regent.

Thus the Queen reached out to the nobleman, forcing him to respond, establishing a way to communicate without seeing each other. She had a room furnished with a large viewing table, and shelves to hold the vellum-wrapped maps. He now had purpose, though still living in seclusion, exploring and extending the known world. She followed him on his path-finding, along the lines he drew, and so she believed she was tracking her lover, travelling vicariously with him, following his traces to the four corners of the globe.

★ ★ ★

For his final journey, Leonardo Capelutto instructed the cook to pack into hessian sacks sausages and cured venison, salt crystals, sun-dried grapes, figs and lemons. Halla packed bedding and a muslin tent, rolled up in a carpet. Eight sets of linen shifts, with pantaloons to be worn under them, were packed for Theodora, as were various small clay jars of herbed creams and lotions to protect her skin from the harsh sun they would be travelling through, and a veil to shield her face from wind and sand. She was given kid leather boots and gloves as well as a jewelled dagger to wear at her side.

There was the possibility that Leonardo's emissary had not reached Balthazar in time, to caution him not to travel. In the event of Balthazar arriving, Leonardo left a letter for him, and gave instructions to the servants that should the old man come they were to settle him into his room and make him comfortable until their return: 'When he sends word that he has arrived, take the wagon down to the crossroads at the edge of town, as usual, to fetch him. Give him all the comfort and ease he is accustomed to. Do not let him leave on his own. I will escort him back to Alexandria with my riders.'

The nobleman, his wife and riders left at dawn of a morning. Leonardo threw a cloak of wool about Theodora; pulled the hood, trimmed with black astrakhan, over her hair, closed it at her neck with a brooch of onyx, seemed not to notice the wetness of her eyes, said nothing. He helped her mount, guiding a leather-booted foot into each stirrup, spreading the cloth of her shift to allow her legs to part across the saddle, tucking the folds of the cloak under it. He placed the reins in her hands, then mounted his own horse.

They set off down the road which led away from the castle, through mist, Leonardo leading his line of mounted men, Theodora riding third from the end, the brass and iron of their saddlery jangling, their horses snorting.

Each of the men carried across his horse a sleeping-roll, water bags and sacks of ground meal. They had tents with them, for the desert climate would be too harsh to sleep outside. Two carried copper cooking pots; one carried a mandolin in a leather box. Each was armed with a musket, a bow and a quiver of arrows, a dagger and a sword. Each wore a cloak of leather and knee-length spurred boots. The riders were men weathered and toughened by the lives they led, as was her husband, though they were coarse and rough while he was refined and elegant. Each rider led a second horse, across whose back were strapped sacks of trade goods.

Behind her, the stained windows on the east side of the castle picked up the first of the dawn light and cast their colours inside. Before her, the world began to unfold. Because she had lived for so long in a sumptuous cocoon of jewelled comfort and artistic beauty, this world beyond the castle, which seemed to stretch on and on randomly, without pattern, again frightened her. She remembered her feelings on her first journey, from the achromatic convent to the castle, as she watched the textures and scale of this outside world change while they moved through it. She was now an accomplished horsewoman, but still she felt she might be consumed by the vastness about her. She hoped that a rider would come by, a lone rider wearing red leggings and velvet jerkin, with a cape about his shoulders and a cap with two feathers clipped to it; a lone rider whose horse would step in with hers and gallop at her side.

★　★　★

Balthazar had arrived at the outskirts of the town a few days before their departure. As he always did, the old man sent his boy-servant up to the castle to announce his coming, so that a wagon might be sent down to fetch him.

But his servant did not reach the castle. The boy was apprehended by a bounty hunter, a chestnut-haired, well-spoken young man dressed in red leggings and velvet jerkin and wrapped in a short cape, who demanded to see his permit to be in the kingdom.

'Sire, I travel from Alexandria with my master, the mathematician Balthazar of Syria. He stands at the crossroads at the northern side of the town, waiting for me to fetch transport. He has my papers, sire. All is in order for me to travel with him in these parts.'

'You say your master is the mathematician Balthazar and that he stands at the crossroads at the edge of town? Where does he plan to go from there?'

'To visit the nobleman Capelutto, sire.'

171

'Is that so? And tell me, does your master have a permit to travel here?'

'Yes, sire, he has papers for us both.'

'Take me to him, then, that I might check upon the two of you.'

But he did not need to check upon their papers. When he saw the old man, dressed in kaftan and skullcap, standing at the wayside, he knew that he had his quarry, and laughed to himself at the simplicity of the hunt. (I did not even have to mount a horse and give chase, he thought.)

'Are you the Jew, Balthazar of Syria?' he asked with dramatic formality.

'I am the Jew, Balthazar, son of Jehuda, exiled from Syria, now resident in Alexandria, mathematician *emeritus* of the University of Alexandria,' replied the old man, taking his travelling permit from his pocket.

'Then I arrest you and this youth in the name of the Queen's Inquisitor. Keep your papers.'

He led the old man and his servant to the office of the Inquisition, in the abbey beyond the town, where he announced to the secretary, 'I have here the Jew Balthazar, who was tried *in absentia* by the Inquisitor and sentenced to face execution by burning at the stake for proclaiming that the sun, and not the earth, sits motionless at the centre of the universe. I submit him to you in exchange for the ransom on his head.'

'What identifies him?' asked the secretary.

'I can identify myself,' interrupted the old man. 'I am the Jew Balthazar, son of Jehuda, exiled from Syria, now resident in Alexandria, mathematician *emeritus* of the University of Alexandria. I journey to visit the nobleman, Leonardo Capelutto. He expects me. Send word to him and he will come for me, and assure you that I am no criminal. If the Office of the Inquisition has brought charge against me, let me see this written charge. Of what am I accused? How can I be charged *in absentia* when I am not a citizen of these parts, but a visiting foreigner and *bona fide* scholar; and when I identify myself as a Jew by wearing this red circle stitched upon my shoulder, as required by your laws?'

'Yes, Jew I see you are. And foreigner you may be. But the law governing crimes defined by the Office of the Inquisition now covers foreigners as well, even if such law does not exist in their own country. If you are indeed the Balthazar named in our warrant, and if you admit to be this person, then your apprehension and arrest are in order. There is no exemption. The Chief Inquisitor will be summoned right away and you may address him directly.

'Take his papers from him. Chain him by the ankles,' the secretary instructed his assistant.

'Send word to the Inquisitor — he is in his suite — that we have his Jew. And then arrange for an armed guard to escort the prisoner to the capital. I know the Inquisitor does not want to detain him here. No one in the town is to know of his capture, so procure a set of black clothes and a hood, and find a covered wagon for his transport.'

He took from the drawer of his *escritoire* a pouch containing five gold coins, which he threw across to the bounty hunter, saying as he dipped his pen into an inkwell, 'I need your name and identity.'

'I am Frederic Montague.'

'Abode?'

'In transit.'

'Present abode?'

'The tavern on the town square.'

'Profession?'

'Travelling actor and playwright.'

'Accompanied by?'

'My wife, Dorothea Montague.'

'Assets?'

'None.'

'How long do you intend to stay in the town?'

'We depart tomorrow at sunrise.'

'Tell me, sire, whether you can help the Office of the Inquisition in another related matter. As a travelling man, and one who frequents taverns and public houses, have you heard tell, either in these parts or further afield, of others who hold demonic views of the universe? Have you heard tell of stargazers, or have any stargazers themselves spoken to you directly of their ungodly practices, or tried to sway you from the Church-given understanding of the celestial bodies towards one satanic and false? Substantial reward is to be paid just for the names of such heathens, there is no need to apprehend them yourself. Just their names will earn you three times the gold you have in your hand.'

Frederic Montague hesitated a moment, and cold sweat broke across his brow. Drawing breath, he said, 'No. I know not of any such person. Nor have I ever met anyone who watches the stars. Except lovers, of course,' he added, trying to ease his fearful tension.

But the secretary was in no mood for frivolity and said coldly, 'Thank you. In that case I have no more questions. Just sign here, then you may go.'

Balthazar put his arm around the boy's shoulder, and looked out of the window at the beautifully symmetrical lie of the abbey's herb garden with its fountain in the centre and outer perimeter of gently swaying lilies. Inside his bag, which had not yet been taken from him, were his telescope and a change of clothes. It also contained a small gift for Theodora: a rock the size of his thumb found in the western desert. It was said, by the nomadic tribesman who had bartered it, to have fallen to the earth from the sky, to have fallen from a shooting star.

Turning to the secretary he said, 'My serving boy is not guilty of any charge. I request his release.'

'That is correct. He is not named in the warrant of arrest. But, as he will no longer be in your employ, his permit to travel as your servant will be nullified. He could be detained by the civil guard for illegal presence in our kingdom. In his own interests — I see he is a mere youth — I will have him taken to the border tomorrow morning and released to make his way home; I trust he knows the route.'

'He will find his way home,' said Balthazar. 'Permit me only to give him what money I have, and his papers.

'I wish to write a letter,' he continued, 'to notify the nobleman, Leonardo Capelutto, of my detainment. He awaits me, and will be concerned at my non-arrival. I wish also to notify the Ambassador of Egypt that I am being detained here against my will, on a false charge, and unjustly sentenced.'

'I cannot permit this. Prisoners of the Inquisition may not correspond with anyone outside the office. I can make no exemption. If you wish to argue this, you will have to discuss it with the Inquisitor himself.'

As he spoke, the secretary, seeing his superior arrive at the door, stood, pushing his chair away behind him, and lowered his eyes briefly. Balthazar turned to face the Dominican, whose hands were tucked inside his robe and whose cool eyes betrayed nothing of his sense of accomplishment.

The bounty hunter pocketed the pouch of gold coins and took his leave.

★ ★ ★

Frederic Montague and his wife Dorothea, travelling players, had arrived in the town some four months before, to recite poetry and short romantic dramas. They had trained in Castille and carried with them a carpet bag of various character costumes: Tristan and Isolde, Romeo and Juliet, Lancelot and Guinevere. They also had with them a leather-bound poem which the young actor had copied out in a beautiful cursive hand.

The players set up their small stage in the town square and over a number of days delivered to the crowd around them ballads, sonnets, romantic verse and also comic pieces. Because they were young and in love, their recitations were rich and full of passion, drawing good audiences who happily threw coins at them.

It was difficult for them to find a place to stay, for the taverns were almost fully occupied by jewellers and dealers in antiquities who had come to buy from the nobleman. He was due back from his travels (though he had been delayed) and had sent emissaries ahead of himself to make known that he was bringing back rare and unusual ambers and precious stones as well as fine porcelain and old bronze pieces. The players could not find a room for themselves, and had to be content with sharing the communal sleeping area of a tavern, generally used by groups of pilgrims but now full of traders' assistants and horsemen.

As usual when the taverns were so well occupied, it was customary for patrons to be served together, at long tables, so there was much conviviality and sharing of stories. Tongues were loosened by mead and ale.

Husband and wife, always listening for tales to inspire their dramatizations, asked one night about the castle that overlooked the town, and its inhabitants. They were much taken by the stories told of the nobleman and his lady. It was said that the noblewoman had an austere beauty; that she was much younger than her husband, who was madly possessive of her; that she was not permitted to leave the castle grounds; that she wore gowns of pure silk festooned in jewels; and that she stood on her balcony, on moonlit nights, staring out across the land.

'She has a string of rubies which she wears about her neck,' announced a man authoritatively, leaning against the table, drinking. 'I'll wager I'm the only one here in the town ever to have seen it. And the only one who ever will.'

'And how might this be,' asked the actor, 'if she has never come down from the castle?'

'Because, young fellow,' he replied, pointing at his artist's smock, 'I've wrapped it round her neck myself. I've painted her likeness. Twelve years ago the nobleman called me up to paint his wife. One hundred and one rubies she has, and I wound them myself, artistically, shall we say, around her beautiful goose-white neck.'

Talk progressed to the nobleman's skill at procuring the most unusual and valuable artefacts, the rarest jewels and precious metals. 'Why, he even went in search of red gold once, with his twin, when they were both young and foolish,' offered the tavern keeper. 'They found the red mines all right, but they also found a pack of savages. Alas, the one was brutally killed — hacked to pieces, they say — and the other came back maimed and without any gold. When their father heard of his child's death, and saw the other's ruined body, the old man died of a broken heart. He's buried there, in the castle grounds. With a garden of white flowers planted for him.'

'How do you know all this?' asked the actor.

'My brother is a rider with him. My brother has seen the scar the nobleman bears across his chest.

'I also know that he has a Jew for a friend; one who is wanted by the Office of the Inquisition, and that this man calls upon him with regularity. There is a high price on that Jew's head. The Inquisitor has tried him *in absentia*, and he faces execution by burning at the stake. He published certain treatises proclaiming that the sun, and not the earth, sits motionless at the centre of the universe.

'But he is elusive. Though he comes

through the town on his way to the castle, no one can describe his appearance. And the Inquisitor cannot have the castle searched, for the nobleman is Cartographer to the Queen. You know how rare such people are. Worth their weight in gold, they are. Add to this the fact that Inquisitor and nobleman are cousins.'

'Why do the servants not sell him out? Or his riders?'

'They are loyal. He has given them their freedom, you know. He had a pack of black slaves left to him when his father died, and he gave each one his liberty, though they chose to stay working for him. The nobleman is known for the care he takes of them. He is a well-liked man. Even here in the town, and among the merchants further afield, he has not one enemy. He gives alms to the poor and supports widows and orphans. Thus, you see, he is a respected man. No one here would betray him.'

'You know a lot,' said the actor.

'Indeed I do. Do you think I just serve ale and leave my eyes to stare into my cups? I'd look out for the Jew myself — I rather fancy that ransom — but the townsfolk would not hold me in good stead if I were to do something against the nobleman, even indirectly; and his riders and free slaves would kill me, as surely as night follows day. I would hate to fall foul of those black men. They have arms like the thighs of bulls. They could wring a man's neck with one hand.'

Later that night, in the soft luminosity of the oil-lamp-lit dormitory, lying against his wife in a narrow uncomfortable bunk, distractedly playing with the lace of her nightshirt while about them snored and grunted the sleeping forms of fellow lodgers, the actor whispered: 'Dorothea, my sweet, here is a new tale to add to our repertoire — the tale of the traveller's wife.

'We have already the two lead characters, the nobleman and his lonely wife; and the minor characters in the form of servants, the Jew and the artist. Enter a third lead — the rogue jeweller. No. Let's not make of him a rogue. Let him be a poor actor, newly married, to a beauty he met in Florence. A beauty who has an enchantment placed upon her by a wicked, jealous maiden aunt. This maiden aunt demands one hundred and one rubies threaded on a chain of gold. But this is an impossible ransom for the handsome performer to pay, because he has barely two coins to his name. By the way, the maiden aunt has her own designs on him.

'Our poor actor presents himself to the nobleman as a jeweller wanting to buy black pearls, and by some skilled trickery acquires the rubies from the nobleman's wife. He undoes the enchantment, poisons the wicked aunt and they live happily ever after, with the rubies, of course, wound around his young wife's neck. How's that?

'All I must do is fathom a way for the actor to get hold of the rubies. How should it be done, my love?' he asked, listening to his wife's measured, sleepy breath. 'What? Am I putting you to slumber with my wonderful tale?' he asked, shaking her gently.

'My love, listen to me. Tomorrow we will pack up our theatre, and I will leave you for a little time; a week or perhaps three. I will hire a horse, for I want to ride up to the castle, to gather parts for a story. You must busy yourself here at the tavern, reciting poems at the tables. Don't fret if I am delayed. I'll leave our bit of money with you, and arrange with the innkeeper that you move from this dormitory and join the maids in their room. I can't leave you sleeping here in a barn full of men without me.

'I'll dress in the Romeo costume, with the velvet jerkin and the leather pants. I will take just one change of clothes, like a man on business travelling light. What say you? Will I cut a handsome figure?

Handsome enough to woo a noblewoman from her senses?'

Before she could answer, he kissed her mouth, then said: 'My Dorothea, my dear wife, I'll stake that before the month is done there shall be wrapped around your fine neck a strand of rubies, a hundred and one of them strung on to a thread, and we will have an extraordinary lovers' tale to add to our repertoire, one quite unlike any other ever written.'

He took off his wedding band of gold and slipped it on to his wife's finger, saying, 'Remind me, dearest, in the morning, before I leave, to take out a signet ring from our costume bag.'

'Frederic,' whispered his wife as he undid the front ties of her sleeping shirt and laid his head on her warm breasts, reaching down and drawing her garment up to her waist, 'it is a fine tale you weave. But I have no need of rubies.'

'Hush. Speak no word,' he said, 'while I make love to you, for you will wake these wretched men about us,' he said and lay upon her, entering her as though on tiptoe, as though balancing on fine cloud, without sound, and kissing her mouth to silence her sigh.

'Perhaps you have no need of rubies, now,

my love. But wait until I give them to you. And wait until I give you more than rubies, but also a heathen Jew's ransom — money enough to put an end to this travelling life and to buy our own theatre, in London perhaps, where I hear there is a great love of drama.

'Will you come with me to London, dear wife?'

'You know I will go anywhere with you, Frederic.'

Outside, the town's night-watchmen walked through the streets, which lay still and content. A horse neighed in the tavern's stable. It was just past midnight.

★ ★ ★

The nobleman and his wife and riders travelled for many days. As on her first journey, they camped in the night openness, she in the tent of muslin, he and his men on sleeping mats, wrapped in their cloaks, under the stars. They cooked food over open fires — grain which they boiled into a porridge; hare or bird which they caught; wild herbs which grew along the way; wine which had a piquancy to it. At the start and end of each day the nobleman brought his wife water in a leather bowl so she could bathe her face and hands, though she missed her servant, for she was no longer used to washing herself. She noted, glancing furtively so as not to seem to stare, that her husband now showed his age. His face was cleaved with lines and scarred by harsh weather and sun. His long black plait was rich with white and silver. How have I not noticed your ageing? she wondered.

Leonardo spoke little to her, asked now and then after her comfort, conversed only with his men at night round the fire while she lay on her carpet under muslin, beneath a star-filled sky. This was because he was used to travelling without talking much. On all journeys he spoke little, and then only to do with the journey itself. For the most part he was silent, reflective and in discourse with his inner self. Now Theodora heard his voice, which was lighter than that of his riders, and she listened to it and to the sounds of the night, which had no castle walls to contain it but which spread on and on to the edge of the earth.

At night in the deep darkness after the moon had set and before the sun rose, her husband would come to her, and she would hide the signet ring under her rug while he loved her body with a sad possessiveness, in the darkness. Still he did not show his nakedness, or enter her. She would hold back her tears until he left her, until he went back to his sleeping mat under the stars. Then she would retrieve the jeweller's ring and hold it to her heart, and let her tears fall, hungering for her lover, wondering why her husband withheld himself the way he did, why he tormented her so.

★   ★   ★

When the nobleman and his twin had first travelled to the red mines, they had gone without a company of mounted men, and with scant knowledge of the miners' ways. They had carried trade goods which they knew to be rare in desert regions — salt, dried citrus, dried apples, certain dried herbs. But what they did not know at the time was that the miners of red gold were a reclusive and jealous tribe, and that no man who entered their territory unbidden left it alive. They should have realized this, because red gold was the rarest of all metals, so rare that a mere ounce could command prices equal to ten pounds of yellow or white gold. Whenever it entered the money exchanges of the civilized world, word soon spread and traders and speculators would bargain fiercely for even the smallest piece; indeed, there was also trade in powdered red gold. To own this precious metal placed one in the company of emperors and kings and dictators. Leaders warred for it; whole dynasties had fallen on its account.

Legends spoke of cities of gold, of solid red-gold citadels, of people clothed in golden chainmail. But none of this was true. The miners hoarded their gold in underground vaults and used it only for occasional trade.

The red-gold miners were said by some historians to be the descendants of a people who had been forced into the desert regions by marauding armies from the east, by plunderers and barbarians who left ruin and fire in their wake. Other chroniclers recorded that the red miners were the descendants of Jews driven out of Babylon centuries before, and that within their rock-hewn city they kept scrolls of the most ancient Hebraic teachings.

Whatever their origins, the miners never returned from the desert to their ancestral lands, but adapted to the heat and desiccating air. They burrowed deep into the agate and amethyst bowels of desert hills, beneath the shifting sands, and lived in cool excavated chambers with walls of jewels that glittered and sparkled in their firelights. These were walls fit for the palaces of kings and popes, but were peopled by those who owned nothing. Fresh water they drew from a deep and ancient fossil-water lake, using it sparingly, for it was to last them centuries; and nourishment they found by seasonally trapping swarms of locusts and migrating birds, drying them and storing them in clay urns. When they occasionally ventured just beyond the border of their territory, bartering their gold with passing, seasoned traders who knew how to transact with these desert men, it was precious salt and simple provisions they accepted.

Their bodies were thin and stunted, their legs often bowed from various deficiencies. They developed cataracts at a young age. Their skin was rough and wrinkled. Life for the red miners was harsh and short and it was spent digging in their mines for a gold that was lusted after everywhere.

Now, on this, his second journey to buy red gold, Leonardo Capelutto knew of the dangers involved in acquiring it, but he also knew how to survive them. His sense of stability returned and the disturbing events of the recent past fell into manageable perspective. Once more he was in control of life. The tangible, physical dangers of travel did not unsettle him.

He felt pleased to have his wife accompany him, and lamented to himself that he had not brought her with him before. He had kept her in their castle, safe from the outer world, preserving the innocence of her convent childhood, shielding her from the cruelty of the outside world as much as possible. But the outside world had come to her and broken her innocence, he now reflected. Perhaps he should have always kept her at his side, travelling with him through dangers that he and his riders could contain or subdue.

Now, the sight of her muslin tent under the white moon and expanse of stars comforted him. In fact, he found having her with him in the wilderness to be erotic. He enjoyed watching her wash from the leather bowl of water, he liked the new smell of her: the smell of dust, of heat, of journeying which now slightly soured her skin. He took strange pleasure in her dependence on him, for she was afraid in the wide landscape they rode through, afraid of the wolves which howled in the surrounding wooded hills at night and of the vast unknown they were traversing. This was not her familiar territory. Wilderness belonged to him and his men. Her vulnerability highlighted the rigours of the journey, its perils. This aroused him.

His riders too found her presence libidinous. They were constantly aware of her; of her company, as a woman, beneath the white muslin tent; of her straight back and swinging short-cropped hair as she rode; of her apparent fragility.

Theodora, in her turn, reflected that her husband's journeys were indeed arduous, and that although he came home burdened with treasures and able to extend the perimeters of the known world, there was little comfort for him, and much danger, away from home.

★ ★ ★

After many days of wearisome riding, the texture of the land began to alter. They left behind the forests and hills of their region and entered the plains. Heat now descended. The nature of the clouds changed: they were no longer voluminous and proud but ribboned and streaked to poignant thinness. The sky seemed more expansive, wider, higher. The heat of the sun grew more intense, sapping the moisture from the travellers' skin, drying their bodies, burning them.

Theodora wore her veil to shield her face, and drew the hood of her cloak over her head to protect herself from the sun. The water in her leather bottle was warm and sickening to drink. She longed for the cool stone floors of the castle, for her bed, for her woman-servant to bathe and oil her.

Gradually they entered the desert. The sands were yellow and hot, yet still some life endured — small, thick-fleshed, thorned plants, which trapped an ancient moisture in themselves, salvaged from the last long-ago rain. Leonardo decided they should travel by night and rest by day under the canvas tents, but even at night the horses were languid.

The desert people were aware that strangers were at the edge of their territory. Scouts skirted the travelling party, watching the line of riders battle their way through the fine, shifting gravel sand. At night they came into the camp — close up to her tent, soundlessly. The horses whinnied, telling of the acrid-smelling men who slunk round them. But the scouts came and went unseen by the nobleman and his men, though his wife sensed them because she was naturally afraid and their presence etched itself into her fear. So she lay awake and anxious until exhaustion stilled her thoughts and she slept.

Finally they reached the red sands, which Leonardo knew not to enter. These were pitiless, dark gravel plains over which sand dunes roamed, rising and falling. No clouds ventured into these parts and nothing grew. Leonardo instructed his men to set up camp. Theodora stayed inside her muslin tent, which was shielded from the intense heat of the sun by an outer canopy the men had erected above it. The horses stood patiently, their heads down, their bridles off to give them some relief.

There was no longer water for her to bathe her face and hands. There was enough only for each to drink one mouthful every hour, and a small amount for the horses. There were new smells here, smells of heat and dust without fragrance or the perfume of flowers.

★ ★ ★

The nobleman set the pattern of trade in motion. At evening he walked away from their camp, a good hundred paces, accompanied by one of his men. They set a bag of salt crystals in the sand, and an empty pouch made from a pig's bladder, then they came back.

At dawn they walked out again. The bag of salt had not been taken. They added another. Next morning the two bags of salt remained where they had been placed. But they had been opened and their contents examined, without any spillage.

Only when five bags of salt had been put down were they taken away by the desert people, and in their place was left, wrapped in the pouch, a handful of red gold nuggets.

Over the next three days Leonardo placed the sacks of sun-dried grapes, sun-dried figs, sausages and cured venison. Soon all his trade goods were accepted and he had, tied at his waist, the pouch filled with red gold nuggets. He now put down a stone jar of honey and their empty water bags. By nightfall, the bags had been filled with pure water and the honey was being shared out, finger-measure by finger-measure, among the miners and their families.

That night the nobleman filled a second pouch with desert sand, believing that among the grains would be some bone particles, that he was reclaiming some part of his twin. His men struck camp and they set off early next morning, back along the route they had come. The horses' loads were lightened now, but Leonardo decided to unburden them further and discarded the cooking pots, all but one of the tents, and all but one of the carpets, leaving them for the miners to take. He kept the sack of dried lemons. Theodora was so drained by the heat that she could not hold herself upright upon her horse but lay heavily against its neck.

The horses battled through the scorched terrain, shaking their heads in discomfort. To reach fresh water as soon as possible, and to shorten their suffering as much as he could, the nobleman altered his course. Instead of leaving the desert the way they had entered, he chose to strike a path to the west, to reach the plains in fewer days. He spread his map and studied it closely, consulting his men. This was not well-travelled territory and not properly charted. He would not normally have chosen to go this way, but the shortage of water gave him no alternative. He decided to head towards a canyon detailed on his map, where a river was shown to flow. They would travel through a gorge, a shorter but more perilous route, until they reached the plains. As they rode the wind hissed, lambasting him, he thought, for claiming back some small particle of his twin. He wanted to shout out loud, to strike at the desert, to curse it, but he did not. Instead he whispered a prayer.

★   ★   ★

The canyon opened before them, contrastingly soft after the desert and beautifully carpeted with white-flowering scrubby plants. Down below, the river ran.

They dismounted, picking their way slowly and carefully down the steep slope, leading

195

their horses. Dislodged stones and rocks tumbled and crashed into the river.

The horses were crazed by the smell of the water. As they reached the valley floor, they pulled loose and raced to drink. Horses and men plunged into the river, clothed and bridled, rippling and disturbing its silver-blue tranquillity.

Leonardo led his wife to a small pool, where he bathed her, soaking her hair, cooling her burnt red face. He stopped her from gulping water and instead trickled it into her mouth. He lifted the gold chain from her neck and looked at her lover's ring, noting sadly, before he tucked it back into her wet garment, that it had no value — it was fashioned from a cheap alloy coloured to look like gold, and already tarnished. He carried her, soaked through, to an overhang of rock, where his men had laid down her carpet and set up her muslin tent. There she was left to sleep and recover.

He decided to remain at the river for a few days, to rest their bodies and feed the horses on the short grass which grew along the river edge. Saddened for his wife, for he knew she would have known by its unrealistic weight how worthless was the ring, he stood at the edge of the river, looking at the reflection of the canyon. She could tell gold from silver, platinum from tin, he had taught her this. Why had she allowed herself to be deceived? he wondered, and then brooded upon the concealment of truth.

One of the men suspended the sack of dried lemons in the river, and when the flesh had plumped out he handed them around to be sucked of their rich and restorative goodness.

They had to keep watch during the night, for this was the territory of desert lions and jackals. They kept their fires burning until dawn; in the early-morning light they caught and roasted fish. Theodora ate hungrily and her strength returned.

On the third night she sat with her husband at the river edge. The swathe of densely packed stars which filled the sky, and the sliver of new moon, were mirrored in the water. They named the stars together, testing each other, and looked deep into their galaxy at the visible planets, discussing the growing of the moon. About them, the sand and river quartz, powdered by wind and time, glittered in the light of their fire. A flock of night-birds flew overhead, reminding her of the first journey she had ever taken, so long ago it now seemed, from her convent to her castle.

She reflected on this present journey, now that the worst of it was over, now that she could look back and view the sheer edges of the danger they had walked through, how closely they had passed to death, how indeed the desert was awesome and splendid. Sitting with Leonardo, a new sense of beauty filled her. Not the beauty of jewels and weavings, nor that of sculpture and paintings or silks. This was a different beauty, one raw and untouched by human hand, one austere and compelling; and she realized that she would want to travel again, that she would no longer be content with the single dimension of her maps, that she would want to enter into their real and tangible terrain once more. Inside her, she felt her lover's child move and the African poem sighed through her mind:

Give me of yourself some part to hold
    within myself and nourish.
Give me of yourself,
    that I may always have thee.
Give me seeds of gwebwa, of chitu-
    patupa, of munzepete;
give me new life after rain.

'Nothing has changed in the red desert since last I was there,' whispered Leonardo, lying next to Theodora in the darkness of her tent. 'Only that the bones of my twin have become sand. How were we to know, young and unwise as we were, that our lives would be transformed for ever in that desert, by our imprudent search for red gold? Shall I tell you now, now that you are here and have seen that endless shifting sea of grains, how I came to bear this scar? How it was that I escaped with my life?'

But Theodora was asleep, and did not hear him tell his tale. She did not hear him say his true name, or how he had known about her in the convent, and how it was that he had come to fetch her to be his bride.

She did not hear him tell how he had been struck across the chest with a sword, and sustained such injury that he too nearly died. But for the expertise of a surgeon, a Jew travelling with a caravan, who found his near-dead body, stitched him with gut and anointed the wound with alcohol, he would have died.

'You see, my love,' he said, 'there have been two Jews in my life. The one you know, our Balthazar, and the other the Jew who carried me back to the plains and left me at a convent, your convent, and so saved my life. There the apothecary nun, your mother, nursed me through the delirium of infection and doctored my wound, reopening it and stitching it into this knotted line across my breast. I lived in your convent for some three years, loved and cared for by your nun, until I was strong and whole again.

'My brother, my twin, older than I but by moments, was the heir to our estate. He was lord of the castle, not I. So when I returned home, repaired by the apothecary, I took his name. I left my own name with his ruined body in the red sand, and took his. Do you hear what I say, my dear one? It was my twin who died, but my twin's name that returned.

'I am not the true heir. I am heir only by some twist of fate.'

He touched her sleeping face, and lightly kissed her forehead. 'A Jew saved me. He could have left me in the sands to die, as any Christian or Moor would have left him, were our places reversed. And a nun finished his work for him. I owe my life to two strangers who happened by at my time of greatest need.'

Leonardo rose and went out into the night, and sat at the fire with the night-watch, his thoughts turning again, as they often did, to the stranger who enters one's life, unbidden, uncalled for, to administer goodness. A hyena bayed.

★　★　★

His death was accidental.

Instructed by him, his men had gone to reconnoitre a more direct way out of the canyon. They had dislodged stones and these in turn had destabilized larger rocks which came cascading down. One struck Leonardo on the temple as he turned towards the sound of the rock-fall.

He crumpled to his knees, with a momentary quizzical expression, then fell to his side, blood trickling from his forehead down the side of his face.

Theodora dropped to her knees beside him, cupping his face in her hands, and shook him, harnessing the hysteria that suddenly clawed at her back, covering her skin with cold sweat. She heard desperate, panting cries gurgle from her throat, watched her hands wipe the blood from his face; all as though she were away from her body and as though time had lengthened, stretching everything into dream quality.

She tore off her chemise and ran to wet it at the river. Then she wiped his face, imploring him to say something, to show her that he was not dead. But he did not respond, only stared up at the sky with still eyes. She called up to his men, waved her arms, screamed for them to come down; her voice echoed back and forth between the stone walls of the canyon so they came bounding down, dislodging more rocks.

They stood around her as she crouched crying over her husband's body. One lifted her away and held her back; another felt for the nobleman's pulse and, finding none, drew his eyelids down, shutting out the sun. Then all knelt and, in unison, beat fist against heart three times, and let out a howl like wolves. Each took his dagger and sliced across his left forearm, drawing blood, which he let drip against his master's breast, as was their way when a rider died.

Theodora had been standing with her husband, her hand in his, when the rocks came down. He had just drawn the gold chain from around her neck and brought her lover's signet ring out from its concealment.

'My love can accommodate the ripples which life must inevitably blow across it,' he had said. He had not asked her to name her lover, nor to tell him what had happened, nor did he question the reasons for her infidelity, for he knew what it was to have a secret.

'I brought a notebook,' he had said. 'That we might write together, and record this journey. But in the desert I gave it no thought. Perhaps tomorrow morning we can rise at dawn and write together.'

Then he had bent down and kissed her tightening belly, run his hands across it, held his ear to it and listened for life.

'We have an heir,' were his last words, as he stood up and stepped back from his wife, turning to the direction of the sound of the rockslide.

★   ★   ★

Donna Theodora Capelutto asked her husband's riders to carry his body into her tent and place him on her sleeping mat.

She drew the tent closed and sat beside him, still clutching her wet, bloodied chemise. As the sun began to set, in the last of its light she drew off his shirt, wet and red with his own blood and that of his men, and saw for the first time the scar that ran across his chest from armpit to armpit, and that he had allowed her to feel but never to look at. She knew it intimately, even though she had never seen it, for she had lived with it all her married life; her fingertips and palms, even her lips, knew its every contour. Each stitch had keloided into a bead; a hundred and one beads ran across his body, like an open rosary; like her length of rubies.

Tentatively she undid the ties of his

pantaloons and spread them open. She undid the ties of his undergarment, and spread this open too.

What she saw made her cry out in disbelief.

Her husband, the nobleman, the traveller, the adventurer, the leader of a band of riders, was not a man, but a woman.

Her mind spun in confusion, throwing up like bits of driftwood in a storm-torn river the pointers which should have shown her that her husband had a concealed identity: the smooth face that he never shaved; the body without hair; his obsessive concealment of himself; his plait of silken hair which he let hang loose when he made love to her.

And he had never penetrated her. She had remained a virgin for the twelve years of their marriage — until the jeweller changed her life.

Who knew her husband's secret? she wondered. Who partnered him in his conspiracy? Did the holy sisters know? Balthazar? Were they all joined together in a drama of deceit? She turned away, retching painfully against the muslin wall of the tent.

Then, without covering what he had taken such pains to conceal from her, she lay beside him, listening to hyenas bark and night-birds cry. Outside, the men spoke softly among themselves around the fire, through the night, keeping watch. One of them plucked at a mandolin and sang.

Theodora cried herself into an exhausted, nightmarish sleep.

★ ★ ★

In the morning she undid his plait, drawing his beautiful long hair forward, and with her fingers combed it down upon his chest. She kissed the scar, ran her finger across each bead of it, stroked a hand down his stomach. She would never think of him as other than a man. Yet now, when she looked at him with proper perception, she saw an exquisite beauty in his finely worked features, coarsened though they were by weather and time. What terrible secret was he taking with him? she wondered. Who had struck him across the breast? Why had he never confided in her? He had taken his secret with him into death.

With care, she knotted the ties of his undergarment, then those of his pantaloons. She covered his upper body with a shawl, then stepped out into the dawn light.

Her husband's men were seated about the last glowing coals of the fire. They rose when she came towards them. She smelt acrid, her eyes were gritty. One of them filled her leather bowl at the river and gave it to her.

She went to the side of the tent and washed, not caring that they saw.

Once, when Theodora had asked Balthazar about prayer, he had told her that he no longer prayed.

'I have distilled all the prayer I have ever been taught or have ever recited into quietness; into a stillness; into just an expression of my homage to creation.

'Prayer,' he had said, 'true prayer, that is, finally becomes reduced to one word. And even that word eventually lifts away. So that prayer is nothing; it is just silence, reverence. Respect. In being nothing more, it is deeply eloquent.'

Now, she found her mind thumbing a rosary of carved beads, seeking the silence.

★   ★   ★

They could not carry Leonardo's body home: the journey ahead was still too long and the heat was putrefying. Concerned that the riders might see his nakedness and learn with scorn of their master's true identity, Theodora had wrapped his cape about him and rolled him in her sleeping rug, tying it with his leather belt.

It was impossible to dig the sands, so the

riders laid Leonardo's body in the overhang, facing the morning star. Theodora placed the pouch of red sand on his breast. The men enclosed him with the muslin of her tent and her carpet, and protected him with rocks and stones so that wild creatures might not disturb him. They picked handfuls of the white flowers and covered their leader's mound with them.

The next morning they struck camp and set off on the long journey home, with Theodora riding third from the end, her veil covering her face. The journey seemed not as long as the journey out, but it was heavy with sorrow. The riders hardly spoke, each deep in his own thoughts, each battling grief by internalizing it and saying nothing, each sealing for ever into the vault of loyalty his suspicions of their master's true identity.

As they rode, Theodora reflected on her life and her celibate marriage, and on her lover's unpeeling of its secret virginal coverings. Her thoughts turned to the Queen and the squares of lace she had sent each year, which now filled an ebony box. The Queen does not know, Theodora realized. Marie-Ursula does not know who my husband really was, she said to herself.

She wondered what she would do now, without Leonardo's strong guidance, without his management of her life. After many weeks, when the castle at last came into view, she wondered if she should take up her husband's role. I have all his skills; he has imbued me with his character; I have only to take up his garments and pull on his boots to fully be him. I will take charge of the castle and all his affairs, she thought wearily, aching from the long and tragic journey. I too can be a nobleman.

Part Three

Who placed the stars,
who kindled their light,
whose doing is the firmament,
who decorates the night sky
so faithfully?

Contemplative Figure

When Leonardo Capelutto was young, he and his twin, spurred on by legends and rumours, and following old maps they had bought from monks and travellers, journeyed to the deserts in search of red gold.

Legend and lore described the miners as astute and careful traders, who never cheated but exacted a payment that they deemed to be sufficient for their gold, having no knowledge of its worth in the world beyond theirs.

But legend had not given instruction in the method of trade they employed; had not explained that theirs was a silent, impersonal exchange, to be enacted over days, and that those who wished to barter gold ought to remain at the edge of the red desert and not enter the territory of the miners. Nor did legend tell that the red miners wished never to meet other races, or to be seen by them.

The nobleman and his twin, valiant and daring because of their youth but already tired and parched by the heat, simply entered the red desert on horseback. What they met with, nothing had prepared them for. From nowhere, as if from the very sands themselves, rose up a dozen or so short, naked men armed with all manner of weapons — swords, lances, thrusting daggers. They rose ululating from the sand and ran frenzied circles around the horses, terrifying the creatures so they screamed and bucked and champed in panic. The wild men slashed at their hamstrings so they collapsed, throwing their riders to the mercy of their assailants, who cut and plunged and stabbed and slashed, then dragged their victims to the edge of their territory, where they stripped them of their weaponry and dumped them for dead, their bones to be a warning to others.

Fate had it that a caravan, travelling east, came upon the bloodied, sandy, barely conscious bodies and that a doctor among them, a Jew trained by surgeons in Alexandria, found the pulse of life in one and, when he strove to assess the injuries, was shocked to see that the body was that of a young woman. His fellow travellers agreed to wait while he staunched the bleeding and stitched the dreadful cut, from armpit to armpit, across the breasts. They made a hammock from one of their tents to carry the scarcely breathing girl, and left her brother's body to be eroded by the sands, rolling him first into a sleeping mat to afford him some small measure of dignity.

They brought the girl to a convent which they knew to be on their route, surprised that she continued to survive the days and nights of travel, surprised that she held on to life.

The nuns, cloistered women bound by vows to perpetual chastity, prayer and meditation, were afraid to accept the body as it was, delirious and smouldering with toxic fever, and so close to death. But the Jew pressed them to put into practice their religion, to make tangible their professed adoration of God.

They would not let the Jew enter their convent to assist them, for he was a man, and not a Christian, and they were afraid of him. So he gave instructions to one of the holy sisters (a herbalist and apothecary, self-trained in the preparation of ointments and potions), explaining to her how to debride and sterilize the wound and impressing upon her the need to keep the patient quiet and still, and for cleanliness.

And then he left and went on his way, praying that the beautiful girl who had looked up at him out of her delirium, her eyes full of pain as he stitched her, would not survive to live with her mutilation, yet conscious that he had done his medical duty in trying to save her life. What was she doing in the desert? he wondered, as he had already done many times and as he would again until the day he died, for he was ever afterwards haunted by her, and by her long black hair knotted through with sand and blood.

★   ★   ★

The apothecary cut away the now putrid bandages and administered powdered mushroom, which was narcotic and which, in steady dosage, kept her patient's consciousness at bay while she worked. She drew out the gut thread, cut away the morbid flesh and the breast tissue, none of which she could save, sucked out with a straw the pus and sepsis, irrigated the wound, drove healing herbal ointment into the flesh and stitched it closed again, from armpit to armpit, with silk thread. Over each of the hundred and one stitches she whispered a prayer, sanctifying her labour.

Then she spread propolis and raw honey across the suture, to contain any infection that might stubbornly colonize the wound site, and bound her work with lengths of linen, feeling well pleased with her endeavour.

Who was this girl, and who had slashed at her body so? How would her womanhood now be, without her woman's form? How would she fulfil herself, the nun wondered as she worked, reflecting that she and her holy sisters were all themselves unfulfilled as women. But they bound their breasts tight against themselves by choice, and shaved their heads, and wore abrasive chafing undergarments to waylay the pleasures for which the body yearned. How would this young woman realize herself, maimed as she now was? Who would take her as a wife?

While the patient had hovered first between death and life, and then between narcotic sleep and dream, the sung prayers of the community of women had washed through her like tides moving with the moon. And she had seen in the distance, between the edge of the water and the land, where the clouds banked up, her twin, on horseback, riding forever into the distance. She had tried to run after him, to free herself of earthly form, but her limbs were weighed down by somnolence, and she stumbled, unable to follow him into the clouds.

When the girl woke, when she realized the extent of her injuries, she asked to be left to die, pushing the nun away from her, sweeping her arm across the bottles of tinctures which stood on the low table at her side so that they fell and broke, spilling their healing properties across the floor. She tried to tear the tight bandaging from her body, so the apothecary had to call for help to hold her patient down.

'How can I go home like this, without my brother and with this mutilation?' the girl cried. 'Leave off with your ointments, leave me alone. Leave this rotting flesh. I have nothing to live for. I don't want to live. Go from me.'

The apothecary sedated her, dropping an opiate tincture on to her tongue; and then she persisted, walking alongside her patient through the dark nights of doubt and fear, holding her when she wept, drugging her when pain became intolerable, administering powders to lift her depression, forcing her spirit to stand upright and wait while the body restored itself, helping her recover the will to live.

Once, while she sponged her patient, the apothecary had asked, 'Should we send word to your home, to say that you are here in our convent, alive? Our gardener will find a boy to carry a letter.'

'No. I cannot let my father see my body raw and swollen like this, or know of the pain which garrottes me so. My father will die if he sees me as this butchered mess.'

'The swelling will pass,' the apothecary reassured her. 'And then the stitches will lie neatly, not angry as they are now, and the pain will one day belong in the past. You will forget it.'

The nun again eased her patient's pain with an opiate, but in smaller measure this time, for she was afraid the girl would become addicted. She led her outside, to rest in the sun. Here she spread a rug on the grass in the enclosed cemetery, where the poppies bloomed. Blackbirds circled the blue sky. The nun left her patient to fall asleep in the sun while she went among the flowers, making an incision down each unripe capsule and harvesting the white latex which bled from them.

★　★　★

Once, when the apothecary went out from the convent walls to the edge of the forest to collect the roots of ferns, to powder and prepare a medicinal tincture, one which she could trickle on to her patient's linen bandaging so it would soak down and soften the scarring, a woodman caught her. He dragged her into the forest and tore off her veil, holding her by her neck so her face reddened then purpled as she struggled for breath. Stuffing her mouth with the cloth of her habit, while the sun splintered through the branches of trees and frolicked against leaves, he tore her garment from her and forced himself into her body, breaking her virginity, breaking her vow of celibacy with an ugly, brutal force. She lost consciousness, only to awake disoriented and sore and with her thighs covered in blood and male fluid.

She made her way back to the convent, where her holy sisters were waiting, and she let them wash her of the woodman's sap which had spoilt her body, then wrap her in a sleeping garment and put her to bed. They kept vigil through the following days and nights, praying for her, chanting, humming their lamentation.

The child that the woodman sired in the body of the apothecary nun was born when the patient was not fully healed, and was kept in a wicker basket in the apothecary's room. One by one the nuns took turns to swaddle and hold and rock the baby. They watched as the apothecary fed the infant from her milk-swollen breasts, a sense of lost womanhood stirring deep within each one of them.

They told the priest who came each Sunday that the baby was a foundling; that the old gardener had stumbled upon the tiny creature, hidden in the forest under mushrooms, wrapped in lily leaves. The priest baptized her in the cold chapel where only one candle burned, and the holy sisters named her Theodora — a gift from God — but knew no surname to give her. They used the name of their order: she was baptized Theodora Poor Clares.

So the baby grew up with holy women in the convent, amidst sung prayer and devotion, living a humble life without other children and without the knowledge of men or the deceits of the world; without knowing the brutality behind her conception. She grew up believing that an angel had conceived her, an angel winged and robed in light, and that her birth to the apothecary nun had been immaculate.

'How is it that so wondrous a child can be born from brutality?' the nun asked her patient. 'She has erased the man's repulsive touch and his smell and his violence, with just the way her eyes smile into mine.'

'Have you indeed forgotten what he did to you? Are you not just hiding his disgusting act from yourself?' asked her patient.

'At night, sometimes, I remember, and feel his hands against my throat, and his terrible weight upon me, but then I get up and take a potion, or one of my powders. And he retreats back into the dark woods, with the wolves.'

'If you had not ventured out of the convent walls, it would not have happened. I am sorry, for you would not have gone but for my needs.'

'Yes, but had I not gone out, I would not have this child to love. We are forbidden to love, as nuns. We cannot love men and we cannot love one another. We cannot touch our own bodies, or look upon them even. Now we all have this child to adore, this beautiful child. From something foul has grown a beautiful white lily.'

★   ★   ★

The apothecary's patient spent almost three years in the convent, recuperating. The young woman slept on a simple cotton mattress in the nun's workshop, watching her at her work with herbs and roots, watching her dry the white latex which she had bled from the poppies, and form it into small squares.

She spent long hours in the cloistered garden, ate simple meals of porridge, spinach, coarse breads and weak wine with the holy sisters, and listened to them at prayer in their chapel. In time her strength was restored. She watched Theodora grow from a swaddled angel into a toddling and adored little girl around whom the nuns hovered and fussed.

'How did you come to be travelling on horseback, as a girl, so far from your home?'

the apothecary once asked.

'My father, Jasper Capelutto, was a traveller. He taught me to ride from an early age, though never on a side-saddle, as women are meant to ride, but with my legs across the horse, bareback even. My brother and I rode with him and journeyed with him, for he trained us in his work. We learnt from him how to travel the world, how to navigate our way. Later we began to draw maps with him, studying whatever old ones we managed to acquire. He groomed us to take his place, and when we reached young adulthood he began sending us off alone, for he was tired and old. In time he assigned certain simple excursions to us, building up our confidence and courage, sending us off with a band of riders trained on the Mongolian plains. We both wore our hair long and plaited, as they did, and our skins toughened and became coarse in the wind and heat. But we were eager and young and foolish. One day we told our father that we were travelling to the glass workers in Venice, that we could go alone without riders, but instead we made our way to the gold miners of the red desert. We thought to bring him back a sack of gold, but instead we have left him to sit alone in his castle, not knowing what has become of us.'

The apothecary asked many questions

about the outside world, about the simple day-to-day fibres which made up life, about everyday happenings, about new knowledge and discoveries.

One day she confided: 'This is a false world, in which we nuns live, locked away from everything and bound by vows as strong as iron, of poverty, obedience and chastity. It is a barren life, here in the convent, as you see, cut off from the world. I would like to leave, but I cannot, penniless and with nowhere to go. I would wish for more for my own child. I would wish that she could know what happens beyond the walls. But alas, she has no father, and no proper name and no marriage dowry.'

★   ★   ★

The day came when, with her health and strength almost completely restored, the apothecary's patient asked to go home. 'I must return to my father, and show him that at least one of his children is alive.

'But I am now neither woman nor man,' she whispered as the apothecary held up a piece of silvered glass that she might see the new landscape of her body. She ran her hand across the plain where her small, young breasts once rose, pert and proper, and where now a line of stitches coursed. She asked that a horse be procured, and a set of men's clothing — a shirt and pantaloons, a waistcoat and riding boots. This the aged gardener helped them do. 'I will be a man, but I will not cut my hair,' said the girl as the apothecary brushed and plaited it so it hung down her back. 'I will take my brother's name, Leonardo, and go home to my father as he. And when your daughter is grown, when she reaches womanhood, I will fetch her and take her into the world and make of her a noblewoman to erase her bastard birth. Have no fear for her. I will free her from your walls.'

'I will wait for you to fetch her, to keep your word,' said the apothecary, leaving the room, for her eyes had become wells and she did not wish to be seen crying. Over the years she had grown close to her patient, stepping out of the boundaries which protocol set between patient and healer, nun and other, and growing to love her.

The young woman returned to her aged father's castle, riding over many days, and in discomfort, on the old work-worn horse the gardener had borrowed for her and for which she would send back a fine mare in exchange. The apothecary had bidden her farewell at the gate, had kissed her mouth, had pressed into her hand a vial of oil distilled from orange; and then gone to her workroom, numbed by grief, where she remained throughout the night, not going to prayer nor to eat. 'How will it be now for me,' she asked aloud, 'without you, whom I have come to love as sister and as friend? Again I will be alone, one among this enclosed group of women, yet nobody really, just a body imprisoned by featureless clothing and blank walls.'

The apothecary's patient found her father broken by worry and sorrow, barely holding on to his life, not allowing himself to die until he heard what blow Fate had dealt his only children. She held his cold hand and whispered into his ear, 'My sister, my twin Loredana, had her life taken by savages, in the desert. I have nothing of her for you, Father, I have brought back nothing of her being and beauty except her long hair.' She wiped the tears which ran down his face, drawing his eyelids shut as deep grief seized his heart and closed it down.

At the side of the castle the new, impostor Leonardo built a walled garden, planted all in white to the memory of Loredana, the girl he once was, and his twin, the real Leonardo. He would keep his secret from all except the apothecary and Halla. In time, in years to come, he would confide in one other.

Word reached the outside world that Jasper Capelutto's child had returned, and when his riders received the news they mounted their horses and rode up to the castle, to pledge again their services (and that of their sons after them) to the noble house.

The Princess Marie-Ursula came, with only one attendant, but the nobleman's child refused to see her and remained locked upstairs. Royal emissaries came after her with letters and gifts, but they too were refused entry, and the royal letters burnt.

Finally the Dominican arrived, to enquire into the well-being of the injured twin, though he was interested only in his uncle's will and to learn what was to become of the Capelutto estate. He listened to his uncle's solicitor read the document, and when he heard that nothing of consequence was left to him, only an annual tithe, he asked to read the document himself. Anger rose up in him as fire, burning him. He grabbed a crystal vase and smashed it to the ground, then marched off, saddled his horse and galloped around the estate, puncturing the flanks of his horse with his stirrups so its eyes were round with terror as it bore him.

At midday, in the dining room, the Dominican confronted his cousin, whom he had not seen since childhood. 'So, the girl is dead — and your body is ruined. How like a cripple you walk, bent forward like an old man. It was foolish, was it not, to travel as you did? It was thought you were both dead, when neither returned. We were preparing to declare you so, and to attend to your father ourselves, and the Capelutto estate.'

'Perhaps so. But as you see, I survived. And bent my body may be for the moment, but each day I straighten more. It is just the scars I bear which are tight and force me forward. My servant oils them; they are softening. I will be straight soon enough.'

They ate in silence.

At the end of the meal they drank the last of the wine, and left the table, making their way to the window. Suddenly the cardinal spun round to face his cousin, and rasped: 'How like a girl you look, Leonardo. Is this the fashion, here among peasants, for a nobleman to wear his hair long down his back? Or have your injuries clipped you of your manhood too? Prove to me you are a man,' he challenged and lunged towards his cousin, grabbing him by the arm and bending it backward, forcing his chest to stretch, so the line of scars rippled in pain and some burst open, staining his shirt crimson.

But the confessor's cousin twisted himself

and broke loose from his foe's grasp, unclasping his dagger, pushing the man back and down against the floor with the blade tip at his throat, drawing blood, and hissing: 'Leave my house, and get off my land, you bastard, or I will kill you.'

It was the Dominican who had the last word. Mounted on his horse, which tramped in agitation and pain as he pulled at its reins, he shouted venomously, 'I wait to see your manhood proved, cousin Leonardo! Let me see who marries your broken body and what you can father with it!' Driving his spurs into his steed, he galloped away.

The nobleman tore off his jerkin and held his palms across his bleeding chest, crouching down in pain.

Cardinal Uriel of Catalonia would bide his time, strengthening his power base and ecclesiastical authority, nurturing his hatred of his cousin, with his sights fixed firmly on acquiring the Capelutto estate and fortune for himself. He did not wish to be forever beholden to the Queen.

★ ★ ★

Sixteen years later, after living quietly and alone with his faithful servants, in which time no one doubted his identity, for he more than

227

proved his manhood, Leonardo Capelutto honoured his promise to the apothecary nun.

He returned to the convent to keep his pledge, not as a girl, not as a wounded person, but as the nobleman who had for many years tithed a handsome annual sum of money to the convent for the care of the apothecary's daughter and for the nuns as they aged. He was indebted to them for his life.

The apothecary's patient came as a nobleman to fetch the nun's child, to marry her and make of her a respected wife, because no one would wed a bastard — not even one sired by an angel.

After Leonardo had taken Theodora away, the apothecary waited for the other nuns to sleep, then unlocked the convent door and went out alone into the cloistered garden, where she watched the moon make its way across the sky until it set. She had told her holy sisters that her patient had a brother who had never wed, and that it was he who had come on horseback with his men to fetch Theodora for marriage and a life outside the convent walls.

The apothecary had been placed in the convent when she was twelve years old, herself born outside marriage, the daughter of an alchemist and his lover. She had taken vows of chastity, obedience and poverty four years later, too young to properly understand them, and had walked out of the convent walls only once after that, when she had gone to the forest to gather mushrooms to treat her patient. She had taught herself to unravel the medicinal properties of plants, making tinctures, testing them on herself. By sending her daughter to someone she knew to be a woman, she thought she would protect her from the brutal hand of men. She was deceiving her daughter, yes, and betraying her too, in a sense. But she was releasing her from the confines of the convent without committing her to a real marriage and the cruel masculine force she imagined it brought with it.

But, more than this, she felt she was herself leaving the walls and travelling out into the world. After her daughter left, in the evenings, after communal prayer, when her holy sisters had retired to their cells, she would take two or three drops of narcotic on to her tongue, then lie on her mat, transported to a place beyond the stars; her sorrow and her sense of loss abated. She loved two people, and could no longer hold either of them. In her opiate dreams she danced with them among swaying summer grasses and purple lavenders.

★ ★ ★

After her husband's riders had escorted her home from the canyon, as soon as they reached the castle, Donna Capelutto called Halla, the Nubian labourers, the beekeeper, the groom, the cook and the house servants to the dining hall where, harnessing her emotions, she broke the news of her husband's tragic death.

Still dressed in her travelling clothes, caked with dust and grime, her hair knotted and sun-bleached, she recounted to her hushed and shocked listeners what had happened. The silence in the room after she had spoken was broken only by the low, faraway rumbling of a storm brewing, and the screeching of Theodora's caged birds.

One by one, each of Leonardo's servants bowed before her, to express their sorrow and to swear their loyalty, which had once been his, to her, and then returned with anxious hearts to their quarters to grieve. Where once was merriment and lightness, sorrow now took hold. The wheat seemed to wail as the wind swept through it; the bees droned sadly as they worked; and the leaves and pods of trees murmured lamentations among themselves.

Outside their cottages, the Nubians beat a

forlorn drum rhythm throughout the afternoon and into the night and following days,
and their mourning songs pulsed into the far
distance, reaching even the edge of the sea to
the north and the start of the desert to the
south. They took a goat and cut its throat,
buried its entrails, drained its blood on to the
earth and daubed themselves with its scarlet.
Then they placed the carcass on a pyre and
burnt it, offering it to their master, hoping he
would find it and take it with him for
sustenance on his journey into the unknown.

Halla felt as though an axe had cut through
her heart. She fetched from her room her
work-basket, and the shirt she was making for
Leonardo, and then followed Theodora
about, carrying it, not wanting to let her
mistress out of her sight in case something
terrible should befall her too. She had only to
finish embroidering a cuff, and then the shirt
would be ready to wear.

Theodora had expected to find Balthazar
comfortably settled and waiting in his suite,
but he was not there. In the hallway, where
the sunlight came through the stained
windows, colouring her clothes with scarlet
and emerald marks, she lifted the still-sealed
letter her husband had addressed to Balthazar. 'Halla,' she asked the old woman, 'did
the scholar Balthazar not arrive while we were

away? I see the letter addressed to him is still here.'

'No, mistress. He did not appear. But nor did the emissary apprehend him. He returned to say that the scholar Balthazar had already left Alexandria; that he was already on the road. The emissary rode the route, always arriving too late at the inns and lodging houses, then rode back and forth again. I prepared the room for the scholar, and it still awaits him.'

'How strange it is, if the emissary did not catch up with him, that Balthazar did not arrive soon after we left. Did you hear anything spoken among the servants? Perhaps one of them heard something in the town.'

'No, mistress. No one went to the town.'

Theodora broke the wax seals of the letters addressed to her husband and glanced through them hurriedly. But they only concerned matters of trade and payment. There was no message from or about Balthazar. Perhaps he had heard from some other source that it was no longer safe to travel, and had returned home of his own accord, crossing paths with the emissary. But then he would have written to notify them, she rationalized. Perhaps there had been a new outbreak of black plague and he had been caught in a quarantined town; perhaps he had crossed the sea to visit his Italian friend, not knowing that Galileo had been detained, only to be apprehended himself. Her concern deepened and she looked through the pile of letters again, hoping also to find one addressed to her personally — a letter of love, a letter of poetry and promise, one scented with aniseed — but there was none.

'Did the jeweller return?' she asked. 'Did he send any message?'

'No, mistress,' said Halla. 'He did not return. There have been no visitors. Only the letter bearers came and left, bringing the correspondence you have before you.' A strange sound came from her throat. An animal sound. Or the sound of water bursting through a tight, closed place.

Theodora now looked properly for the first time since coming home into her serving woman's grief-riven face and stretched out her hand to her, taking her into her arms, saying gently, 'Do not weep, my Halla. We will live together, you and I, and keep everything as it always has been, so that his spirit finds its way about, here in his own home. It will come back from the desert. It will be here again. Come, Halla, let me take you to your room. You must rest awhile.'

But the old woman refused, for she did not

want to be by herself. She was afraid of her thoughts; was afraid that the face of her mistress's lover would show itself, would leer at her from the dark passageways and taunt her to reveal what she knew; she was afraid to accept the truth of her master's death. 'Let me stay with you, mistress. Let me be with you. I cannot be alone,' she said. 'Let me oil your body, for it will calm my soul; let me caress you, for it will still my heart.'

'Later, later tonight,' said Theodora, leading Halla to the kitchen, where she poured two glasses of sweet wine. 'Drink, Halla, still your heart with the wine.'

★   ★   ★

The next day, Donna Capelutto paid the riders in gold coins, as was always their due. She gave them each a nugget of red gold, in payment for their loyalty and long service to the nobleman, keeping back the rest — enough to fashion a simple choker for an empress, and still some over.

Then she drank wine with them, and they raised their glasses to the nobleman, whose body now lay at the mercy of wind and sand and time. 'Call upon us, Donna Capelutto,' their leader said, 'if you have ever a need of us. We remain at your service, as we served

234

the nobleman, Leonardo Capelutto.'

They saddled their stallions and she watched them ride off home, where they would share their tales over their fires, of how the nobleman's wife had become a rider like themselves; of how she had ridden the most perilous of journeys and survived. She watched them disappear into the distance, then, followed by Halla, went up to her husband's room, closing the door behind them.

Everything was in its place, as always. They lit candles and an oil lamp. Halla sat at the window. Theodora walked about, with heavy heart, seeking Leonardo, hoping he would come down the spiral stairs from the viewing room and take her in his arms, wrapping her again in the scent of sandalwood. She lay on his mattress, looking up at the ceiling where the angels still smiled and the figures of legendary gods and demons battled good and evil. Perhaps he would step in from the balcony, and drop his garments to the floor to show her his naked body; and it would not be the mutilated woman's body she had seen in the canyon, but a body like that of her lover, bronzed and whole and in full view to her.

She searched her memory for the sound of bells and the murmur of prayer and the cadences of holy women singing; finding the adorations far away, beyond the sun and moon, beyond the last visible planet, beyond the outer reaches which Balthazar had drawn for her.

The child within her stirred and suddenly she was overcome by a sense of utter loss as quiet sobs seized her body. She cried until she fell asleep, waking in the morning to find her faithful servant sitting beside her.

'Halla,' she whispered, 'do you know my husband's secret?'

The old woman — for whom, over time, the kind lacings of acceptance and forgetfulness had concealed from her memory the horror, so many years before, of Loredana Capelutto's return home, on horseback, alone and without her twin, thin, weathered, deepened, changed — now looked back at the past.

On that day, Halla had rushed up the stairs to the old nobleman, Jasper Capelutto, where he sat at his balcony looking out across the lands. 'Master,' she had exclaimed, 'Loredana is home!'

She had hurriedly opened up the twins' room, which they shared, and brought hot water up, preparing towels and clean garments, while Loredana took the stairs, solemnly, to her father's quarters, holding him as he wept with joy to see her, and breaking the terrible news of her sibling's fate.

Later, when Loredana undressed before her faithful nurse, tearing open the gardener's jerkin and throwing it down, unlacing the gardener's shirt, baring her chest, revealing the river of scars which ran across the terrain of her breast, she said, 'Let me show you, my Halla, my suckling nurse, let me show you how I am now changed, let me show you the cord of knots that has been carved across my body.'

Halla had stumbled, as she came towards Loredana, reaching out to the scars, touching them, then letting out a wail, a piercing score into the silence, which disturbed the birds nesting in the eaves, and carried out into the lands so that the gardener turned his head.

'Put away my old clothes, Halla, and then sew new garments for me. Sew me clothes for the new person I am, and help me lay my past to rest. From now I am your master, not mistress; from now I am Leonardo Capelutto. Loredana is dead. And do not weep, I beg you, for it will tear my heart to hear you. Let us just begin together this road forward and not let our grief overpower us.'

With the gardener, they had seeded the white garden and planted bulbs, jasmine, lilies, jonquils, roses. Then Halla had set herself to making pantaloons and boleros, high-collared shirts, shirts with pleated sleeves, laced jerkins, stitching and embroidering them with love. From then on she faithfully served Leonardo Capelutto and mourned the death of his sister, keeping her tears for the night so they would not be seen. In time, for her, the deception became true.

Now, when Donna Capelutto asked her to remember the past, asked her to face the shadows of long ago, she could remember only two things.

'Yes, I know my master's secret. Years ago, when he was a youth, he played the lyre and he sang. He had a sweet voice, like that of a bird. But after his journey, after that journey which stole his sister, and at his father's death by grief, he smashed the lyre and sang no more.'

★　★　★

Donna Capelutto did not leave her husband's room, but remained there to smell the last of his presence as the fragrance of sandalwood slowly retreated, and to be among his books and pens and instruments of navigation. She spent long night hours on his viewing balcony, looking out at the stars; she slept on his mattress. Halla kept vigil, harbouring her quiet grief, sitting in her chair, embroidering the cuff of Leonardo's shirt, dozing on and off, waiting to do Theodora's bidding.

Now her mistress asked for pressed fruit juice, and read again the letters that had arrived, addressed to the nobleman. Among the promissory notes and bankers' statements was an order for bolts of raw silk and another for jade artefacts.

She looked through their maps — each was rolled and stored in its own tube of vellum — and opened one depicting the silk route. Even though I know the way, she thought, for you have described to me its every step and I have drawn the Queen's copy myself, I will follow your chart, this the one your own hand drew.

She spread the map on his table, her eyes awash as she looked upon her husband's fine calligraphy, at his inked mountain ranges and rivers. She opened a second map, one depicting the islands beyond the South China Sea. This she placed on top of the first, weighing down the corners of both with rocks of amethyst.

She fetched his notebooks from the shelves, thirty-seven booklets in all, and placed them in sequence along the table. 'I will read them all again,' she said aloud. 'I will read them, my husband, though I have read them so often and know them as if I had myself travelled their routes.'

She took out sheets of writing paper and pens, uncorked a bottle of ink and wrote six letters. The first was to Balthazar, to break the news of Leonardo's death and to enquire after what had happened to him — why he had not completed his journey — and to seek reassurance after his well-being. She also warned him, though he surely already knew, not to travel through Christian territories. She wrote that she was carrying a child, that it was due to be born within a few months and that she longed for his presence, for she felt so alone.

She replied to the two merchants who had ordered silk and jade, accepting their requisitions, asking each for a promissory note covering twenty gold sovereigns to validate their instructions, and confirming that their goods would be delivered within a year and a half. The fourth letter was to the goldsmith who had ordered the red gold, and in this she said that the gold had been impossible to procure. She returned his promissory note. The fifth was to the Queen, advising her of the tragic death of the nobleman but assuring Her Highness that she was well able to take her husband's place as Royal Cartographer, if the Queen was willing to accept her work.

She addressed the sixth letter to the apothecary nun.

Beloved and holy mother,

Forgive me for intruding upon your privacy and entering, unbidden, your closed cloisters by means of this letter.

I send tidings both sad and joyous.

My husband, the nobleman Leonardo Capelutto, was killed in a tragic accident while travelling in the desert regions. And I am with child. Therefore my thoughts and needs turn to you.

Although my baby, due to be born at the start of winter, was not sired by an angel winged and robed in light, as I was, I wish for it to have the same protective upbringing as my own, and for it to grow up with you, in your holy dwelling and surrounded by prayer.

Will you permit me to bring the child, together with a suckling nurse, to live with you in your convent, among your sisters and my other mothers, until it comes of age, so that it might learn about silence, and the inner journey; and how to extract the essential essences of herbs and flowers; and how to distil prayer in a place where no evil dwells?

In the same way that my husband supported my upbringing in your convent, I will tithe the same amount, paid always in gold, at the start of each winter, for the keep of my child. And as the nobleman Capelutto fetched me, so will I collect my child, in the nineteenth year of its life, to take up its noble title, and to learn about the outer journey and about life in the world.

I wait in anticipation to hear that I may bring my baby to you, trusting that you will honour my request and, in so doing, permit me to enter your convent door and to see you once again.

I remain, yours sincerely

Donna Theodora Capelutto

She folded the letter, lit a pencil of red wax, let a drop fall on to the paper and pressed her husband's seal into it. She sent word to her husband's riders, informing them that she would continue the nobleman's work of travel and procurement, and as Royal Cartographer. If they wished to accompany her, they should be ready to travel after the winter, when she would journey to the east, via Alexandria to visit the scholar Balthazar, and then onward, first to obtain silk and jade, and then to purchase black pearls from the islanders beyond the South China Sea.

Then she took to her room, where she waited as her body swelled with her lover's child. Each morning and evening, Halla bathed her and oiled her and rubbed the stretching skin of her belly with soothing lotions. She brought her mistress fruits and warm milk, and rice porridge with honey. She massaged her feet and wrapped cool cloths about her swollen ankles. She rubbed oil into her mistress's firm breasts and blossoming nipples. She readied lengths of cotton for the birthing; began knitting swaddling blankets and small robes of the finest lambswool. From the storage cellars Halla brought up a crib, carved from beech and spacious enough for twins; and from the town she summoned a wet-nurse to be ready to help with the suckling of the soon-to-be-born infant.

'Halla, will it be you who helps me with my birthing?' asked Theodora. 'Will you lift my child as it comes from my body? It should not be a stranger who does this for me.'

'It will be me, mistress, who first holds our child. I will wrap it in swaddling clothes and hold it to your breast.'

'I am afraid, Halla, of everything that has happened and of what lies before me now. I am afraid of what is to happen to my woman's body.'

'There is nothing to fear, mistress. Only that your body will heave, like the earth splitting. You will feel you are moving rocks from within yourself. That is all. And then we will have a baby to love. And the spirit of my master will have a child to carry his name.'

★   ★   ★

Far away in the convent, Donna Capelutto's mother, the apothecary nun, asked the emissary to wait at the gate for her reply. Then, alone in her work-room, she broke the seal of the letter he had brought to her. She had always known that there would come a letter one day, written in script other than the nobleman's. But still it shocked her to hold it, for she knew that truth was now knocking at the door of her soul.

She read her daughter's epistle slowly, once, twice and a third time, tears clouding her eyes. The hold she had placed upon her heart to stop it from bursting with grief when she had sent her child away now loosened itself. The binding she had knotted around her act of deception now came undone. Her daughter had finally come to know of the sham upon which her marriage and freedom were based. But more than this terrible undoing — her daughter was carrying a child. She had betrayed the nobleman, her husband, and lain with another.

Anguish poured from the apothecary's heart, seizing her throat, almost choking her. She steadied herself, and forced herself to face the two betrayals which now danced before her like two courtesans with gaudily painted faces and richly attired bodies. They danced, the Betrayed and the Betrayer, mother and daughter, garbed in theatrical satins, jewelled in glass beads, daubed in cosmetics and fragranced with cheap perfumes.

She took paper, quill and ink and wrote her reply, saying simply that the apothecary was no longer alive and that the convent did not house infants, signing it with the name of the Mother Abbess. She folded into the page a sprig of rosemary, sealed it and gave it to the emissary. Then she returned to her work-room and the hidden drawer where she kept the reddish-brown, heavy-scented opium she extracted from the red poppies that once grew wild in the convent burial ground (and which she now cultivated). Carefully preparing and taking a dose, she lay down on her mat and allowed the narcotic to carry her into the dream space where lilies grew and where marshes harboured plumed birds and huge insects; where a curtain of silk softened everything, giving it the appearance of haze on horizon.

★　★　★

The emissary carried the apothecary's letter of reply back to the castle far away where, sitting on her balcony, Theodora now faced the realization that her lover would not return. But, not wanting to admit to his deception, she speculated that perhaps some harm had befallen him. Perhaps he had spoken publicly about the true state of the night sky; perhaps he had not realized how terrible this secret knowledge was which she had disclosed to him, had shared it in a tavern with strangers who betrayed him. Perhaps the Dominican's net had ensnared him. Within her, stirring with the same movement of her unborn child, the epic poem led her along to its inevitable conclusion.

See how I wait for thee, kind sir, here
  beneath the majanji tree,
rich and heavy with ripened seeded fruit;
  bursting with life.

*Do you come? Is that your drummer in
  the distance,
playing love like music? Is it you,
  Chilangulangu,
singing love songs in the wind and
  calling me?*

She closed her eyes. She knew every word of
the epic. It was carved upon her heart.

*I come, yes! I, Nkwazi, come winged as
  wind though never more in flesh,
I come, crying out your name.
Wait, mistress! Wait beside the water,
  wait at the small spring;
wait at the dawn and in the evening
  time.
For there I will be, always, watching,
  loving thee.*

By day, as she listened to the sounds of life
on the estate, she watched the distant horizon
and the twisting road that led past the town.
By night she watched the planets rise and set,
holding her small rosewood rosary. On the
table at her side she kept her husband's
notebooks and Marie-Ursula's ebony box
filled with small squares cut from lace.

She knew how to wait. But now her waiting
was different, it was refined and patient. It

247

was the waiting of maturation — pressed sap fermented to wine; nectar transformed to honey; dream and illusion metamorphosed into reality; the waiting for the child taking form within her.

When the chill of early darkness settled, Halla would call her in, rub her lower back and put her to bed, drawing the bedclothes up around her, closing the fine curtains of the bed. Then she would sit beside her mistress, dozing on and off as she kept watch over the apothecary's daughter, while up from the Nubians' cottages drifted the sounds of reed flutes and drums.

In the darkness — cut by a single candle — as Theodora listened to the labourers' soothing songs, and just as she surrendered to sleep, it would be her husband who came to her, stepping out of the shadows, not her lover. The nobleman would stand at her bedside, translucent, in his embroidered shirt and pantaloons, his long hair loosened and hanging down to his waist, with the scent of sandalwood all about him. Theodora would reach out to him, to tell him that she had let a purveyor of jewels enter their secret world, that he had enchanted her with poetry and good literature, enthralled her with his eloquence and wit, and that she had succumbed to his fine love-making. The nobleman would smile reassuringly at her, and take her in his arms, walking with her into her dreams, while behind them followed Balthazar, with an angel at his side.

★　★　★

On the morning that Theodora's waters broke and spilt down her legs, when the first heavings of birth seized her body, she made her slow way down the stairs to the white garden, pausing for breath each time a contraction rose, clutching at her belly, panting in pain as she waited for it to settle.

There were no blooms now, only green foliage and seed-pods. Theodora, with fountain water splashing her face and wetting her hair, hung the gold chain on which was threaded her lover's ring around the neck of one of the marble water-nymphs. Then she kissed the leather-bound poem and placed it in the pond, where it immediately released from its pages the ink of its elegant lettering, like black blood, into the water. She watched a golden carp swim through the colouring which had once been fine script; watched the folio sink down among the roots and stems of water-lilies.

She closed the door to the garden and asked a Nubian to help her walk, leaning heavily against him, both of them stopping when she needed to breathe against her pain, so that the strong smell of his sweat enveloped her.

'Child!' exclaimed Halla when he brought Theodora in, 'what madness is this? What has happened? Why are you wet? Oh, the baby! The baby's life! Help me, help me get her upstairs!'

The Nubian lifted Theodora and carried her, following the old woman, and placed her tenderly on her bed, without looking around the room, without looking at the furnishings, without looking into his mistress's eyes.

Halla undressed Theodora and dried her hair, then wrapped her in a gown as the rhythm of birth deepened and intensified, like a storm at sea. 'Halla,' whispered the noblewoman, 'I want you to lock the garden. Ask the farrier to make a bolt and to lock the gate. No one is ever to enter there again.'

'I will do so,' said Halla, giving her mistress a leather strap to bite against.

Brother Matteo, who had been called that morning, waited outside Theodora's door to baptize the child of the nobleman.

★　★　★

At that same moment, in the capital, at the royal palace, the Inquisitor sat before Queen Marie-Ursula.

'Highness, it is time now to take action regarding the Capelutto estate,' he said firmly, wringing his hands then stretching out his fingers and touching the emerald of his ring. 'It is some time since you received notification from his widow of the nobleman's death. I remind you that in terms of his father's will, because he died without an heir, his estate is to revert to the Crown.

'I have had prepared a certificate for transfer of ownership,' he said, placing on her desk a gold tray upon which lay an inkwell and quill and, ready for her signature and seal, a document written in illuminated lettering. 'With your permission, Highness, I would like to establish a new abbey there, to create a retreat for myself, to celebrate the work I have accomplished with Jews and those who trespass on holy ground. With your consent, Highness, we will found a new order there, and give my own name to it.'

'What would become of Donna Capelutto, if we were to affix the property?' asked the Queen.

'Once the abbey is established, with monks abiding there, it would not be in keeping for the widow Capelutto to remain living among them, though she has experience of religious life. I suggest we send her back to the convent where she was reared.'

251

'I would do this reluctantly,' said the Queen, 'for it is through the Capeluttos that the borders of my empire have reached as far as they have. Leonardo and his wife have mapped all the new territories. While he lived, I accepted his refusal to attend the court and his preference to live in isolation because his work was, and remains, immeasurably priceless. No other kingdom has maps such as ours. They are invaluable and can never be replaced.'

'It is God's will and will be in God's name, Highness, that we establish this new order with the Capelutto fortune, precisely to show gratitude for the expansion of your territories. The Capelutto widow, barren and childless as she is, will be well cared for in her old convent. We might even make her Abbess and permit her to have servants, even furnish her own private quarters so she loses not sense of her high position. We must not think of ourselves or of our sentiments towards others in such a case, Highness. We must think of God, and our service to God, and our devotion to God, and display our gratitude in an appropriate manner. The new abbey will be dedicated to His great glory. It will be consecrated to coincide with your thirty-fifth year on the throne.'

'Allow me some time to think upon this,' said the Queen.

'Highness, to help you, take it as a mark of God that this is His will. God has shown you this with a very simple sign. He has not blessed the Capelutto family with an heir. The blood-line stopped with Leonardo's death. Had there been an heir, we would have known God's will was to continue the Capelutto heritage and built our abbey elsewhere. One might reflect, too, on the nobleman Capelutto's choice of bride. He chose not to marry someone high-born and of his own class. By selecting a lowly born person, one without proper parentage and without social standing, he showed no ambitions for his family name, and God in His all-encompassing wisdom has seen fit to end the lineage.

'I will take my leave now, while you pray alone for clarity on this matter. In the meanwhile I will attend to the more pressing problem of Capelutto's freed slaves. There is living on his estate a band of black servants, once his father's slaves, and their descendants, to whom he granted freedom and who he said are baptized. Through these years that I have been clearing your kingdom of demonic influence, he has permitted pagan savages to invite the Devil every night to his property, and to entertain the Devil not only with vile music and manners but also with sacrifices human and bestial. We have in our very midst a bed of evil; we have a doorway to Satan's banqueting table, in our own country, and the doorman has been none other than my relative and the man you employed and protected.

'I am tasked now with rounding up those savages and condemning them to the flames of hell. I will dispatch them to their master, Satan, without delay. This I do for you, Highness, and for my love of the divine.'

The Queen's confessor bowed slightly and left the room, calling to his secretary, who had been waiting outside, to follow.

★ ★ ★

On her own, in her suite, Queen Marie-Ursula kissed the gold crucifix which hung from her neck, lifted the document which her Inquisitor had prepared for her signature, and read it as she paced upon the silk-carpeted floor, steadying herself on a gold cane. Should she allow the Capelutto estate to become religious ground, she wondered, or should she leave it as she knew it, and as it had always been — a place where she once laughed and played and made love under the stars?

Her thoughts turned back to the one and only day the nobleman had set foot in the palace, and met with her, in this very room, upon this same woven spread of Chinese workmanship, to ask her permission to marry a young, convent-reared girl, so as to have a companion, for he was beginning to find his loneliness unbearable.

He had bowed before her, to honour her, but had not knelt. He had lowered his head in respect, but addressed her simply as Maru, not Highness or Majesty.

'How is it that you wish to marry now, and someone of lowly birth at that? How is it that you chose to remain alone all these years, refusing me, leaving me also alone and unwed, just because of your disfigurement, when I loved you so? Show me the mutilation which kept you from me,' she had said. He had unbuttoned his shirt and drawn it back. She had stepped towards him, stretched out her lace-gloved hands to run them across the beaded scar, but had not touched it, saying only, 'It is no worse than my purple, shrivelled leg and bent foot.'

'Maru,' he had said softly — so softly that the Queen had to step closer to hear him — 'I am Loredana, not Leonardo. It was my

255

brother who was killed, not I. Your lover was slain in the desert and his body claimed and corroded by sands. I have lived a charade all these years, acting a role not mine, playing a part not my own, pretending, disguising, deceiving. I have been reduced to a mere actor.'

There was silence in the room. From outside came the castrato chorusing of cicadas and crickets. But inside a suffocating quietness settled, concealing everything.

The Queen came close and took his face in her hands, saying, 'Is this why you have not let me cast eyes upon you through all these years; why you hide yourself from me so cruelly? I have not seen your expression since we were young.'

She walked to the window and stood awhile, then turned back to look at the nobleman. 'You could have told me; instead you deceived me. I loved you both. Indeed I love you both still. Never a day goes by that I do not think of you, brother and sister, my only friends. I would have supported and comforted you. I would not have betrayed your charade. Indeed, I could have joined you in it. We could have married, you could have become King. We could have play-acted together all these lost years, could we not? Instead we have both lived alone.'

'No, Maru, I could no more have been King than a beggar. I have spent these years torn in spirit, crazed in mind. The travelling stilled me. The long days on horseback, the long nights under unknown skies, were balm to my soul. Travelling with my riders, who expected nothing of me save leadership, forced me towards sanity. If I had come to court, I would surely have gone mad.

'But now, now that my heart is quiet, the loneliness within my castle corrodes me. I cannot call upon my riders to live with me; they have their families and homes; my servants are as distant as servants must be. I am alone in my castle, living with marble statues which do not speak, and among cherubs and angels spread across my ceilings and walls who never change their expressions, and with the portraits of my ancestors who never alter their postures. I need a companion to share my life now. My body needs to be held, and I wish to hold someone. I need tenderness, and to feel the flesh of another against mine.'

'Who is this girl you have chosen?' asked the Queen. 'Hers is not a name I know. Is she born of nobility? You say she lives with nuns; was she perhaps the illegitimate child of someone high-born?'

'She is the child of a nun. She has no father

and no dowry. She has no name. But she is educated. Because she has lived in seclusion, she will feel liberated when she comes to me; yet, knowing nothing of the world, she will not yearn for what I cannot offer her.'

Queen Marie-Ursula was silent for a while, then said, 'If you had told me of Leonardo's death, I could have mourned him properly.'

'If I had told you, Maru, what would have become of me?'

'You would have had my friendship, instead of this terrible aloneness you inflicted upon yourself. And I at least would have known my beloved's true fate. If I had known, I would have been sensitive to his spirit seeking me, for surely his soul did not stay there in the desert. Surely his soul came home to me, but I was not attentive, thinking you were he.'

They had stood before each other, then stepped into an embrace, as though about to dance, but they did not dance; instead they stood still, holding tight to each other, both weeping, so that the tears of one washed into the other's grief, like snow-melt entering a swollen river. 'Forgive me,' whispered the nobleman.

The Queen stepped back from him, searching his face for that of her lover, wiping the tears from it with her gloved hands. She loosened his plait and brought his hair forward so it fell heavily, and she took a handful and kissed it.

'Take the young woman as your bride. You have my blessing. I will tell no one of this masquerade,' she said.

'Never invite us to the palace. Honour my chosen solitude, I beg of you,' he implored.

'I have honoured it until now,' she responded.

When the nobleman left, the Queen had watched from her window as he leapt upon his horse — caparisoned in the burgundy and cream colours of the Capelutto coat of arms — and rode towards the walls of the palace grounds, his long loose hair blowing in the wind. At the ornate gate he had turned to face her window, knowing she was there, but not seeing her through the heavily laced curtaining. He had drawn his sword and lifted it into the air, saluting her; and she had bowed her head.

Now, remembering that meeting, the Queen tore the Inquisitor's document in half and threw it down. She reflected on the nobleman's freed slaves and their inevitable fate at the hand of her confessor. She thought about the nobleman's wet-nurse, who must be an old woman now; drew from memory the black men reaping wheat and picking fruit; remembered their melancholic songs which caressed the nights.

No, she thought. They can be no more pagan than I; and she rang the bell which summoned her secretary.

★ ★ ★

As night fell, the cry of a newborn baby rang through the Capelutto castle. In the kitchen, Nubians, servants and riders raised cups of mead, and the cook cut slices of meat pie and mulberry tart. A rider saddled his horse in readiness to take word to the royal court.

'How strange are the workings of God,' commented the cook, wiping her hands on her apron, 'that our master should die before his long-wished-for child is born.'

Upstairs, Halla gently bathed the baby in warm oiled water, wrapped him in the linens she had prepared and placed him in her mistress's arms.

'I will name him Leonardo Balthazar Capelutto,' said the noblewoman. 'Is that not a fine name, Halla?'

'Oh yes, mistress, there can be none finer. And he will grow to be as good a man as his father, and courageous too,' said the faithful old woman, beaming as she opened the door for Brother Matteo, crossing herself. 'Brother Matteo, we must send word to the palace, to let the Queen know that a son has been born to Donna Capelutto. A rider is ready downstairs to take your message.'

'Indeed, yes, Halla,' said the monk. 'Go down to him and send him on his way, without delay. Let him tell the Queen that the noblewoman Donna Capelutto has been delivered of an heir. But let me baptize the infant right away, and bless his life. Alas, that his father did not live to see him.'

Outside, steady drumbeats rose in ecstatic celebration, their sound dancing with the spiralling breath of reed flutes.

At the Office of the Inquisition, Cardinal Uriel of Catalonia signed the papers for the arrest of the Capelutto freed men, their wives and children. He ordered that they be brought to the capital in chains, to be publicly displayed for seven days and then burnt alive at the stake for practising pagan and satanic ritual and for being agents of the Devil in his work of evil. But these warrants of arrest would be nullified by Queen Marie-Ursula in her first and only act of defiance against her confessor.

* * *

In the immediate sky the earth's moon and the moons of Jupiter journeyed formally around their planets, in exact and measured time; while Venus, illumined by the sun to a jewelled brightness, danced with her brother planets through nocturnal black velvet.

Down below, far away, a hot wind stirred across white flowers blooming in a desert canyon, in celebration, it seemed.

In a fabulously ornate reception room, a queen instructed her secretary to make preparations for her to visit a recently widowed noblewoman, newly delivered of child, that comfort and sisterly support might be given to her in this lonely time of need.

And in the library of his home in a better quarter of London, seated at a round oak table and working under the light of oil lamps, their flames long and unmoving, a young playwright took out his paper, quill and ink to begin his next dramatic work. He tenderly touched the petals of a sprig of jasmine, arranged with white roses in a vase at his side, as he conjured up his cast of main characters. They all stood before him, ready to take up their roles, waiting for him to name them and to garb them with various passions and vices.

The first to accept life was a noblewoman, and a puckish one at that, beautifully costumed in an indigo dress, laced at the bodice, a single diamond hung by a thread of gold at her *décolletage*. The second character to respond to the playwright's call was a beguiling travelling purveyor of jewels; the third a Dominican cardinal whom the playwright would model on the Spanish Grand Inquisitor, Torquemada; the fourth was someone who had once lived, the Italian genius Galileo, though he would not play a prominent role: he would merely bring with him his discoveries and propositions to challenge the status quo of the known universe. In the shadows stood a nobleman and an astronomer-mathematician, both waiting to be summoned, though the playwright was not yet ready to script them. They were to be the more complex of the main characters, with some scores to settle, so were left to wait awhile.

For his fiction, the playwright chose not to name the country in which his tale unfolded, because it was to be a story that could happen anywhere and at any time. It was to be a story about intolerance and persecution, an intrigue of love and deception, and an exposition of the ease with which one could betray and condemn another. He set his story at a historical crossroads, where the armies of ancient empires had once marched and conquered, and then left their ruins. He chose to unfold his tale at a time when the

Holy Roman Church rained fire upon other faiths and cultures, burning books and testaments, scholars and beliefs, in conflagrations which for ever after cast their dark ash over the light of civilization.

As he dipped his quill into black ink, drawing the nib against the rim of his inkwell, he looked across the table at his lovely wife, and at the sparkle which the lamps' light threw against her crimson-jewelled necklace, wound five times around her neck. She smiled sweetly at him, shuffled a pack of cards and set them down to play a game of Solitaire. He paused for a moment, thinking he could hear steady drumming far off. A quick shiver of cold ran through him as he began to write, his tale flowing unhindered like a mountain stream.

Far, far beyond, in unnamed, unknown galaxies, suns held planets of their own in place, like circles of galactic rubies, choreographed to an eternal, exquisite, silent dance.

Glossary

Almaden Greatest mercury mine in the classical world; two hundred kilometres from Madrid and still mined in modern times. Heavy mercury, when combined with burning sulphur, produces cinnabar

chilangulangu (Shona) Nyasa lovebird

chitupatupa (Shona) *Gnidia kraussiana*; yellowheads

gwebwa (Shona) *Podranea brycei*; Zimbabwe creeper

kaross (Khoi) Cloak or blanket made of animal skin

mezuzza (Hebrew) Jewish doorpost symbol. An outward sign of God's presence and a sanctification of the dwelling place

munzepete (Shona) *Boophane disticha*; tumbleweed

munzvirwa (Shona) *Vangueria infausta*; false medlar. Deciduous tree widespread in woodland and particularly characteristic of granite kopjes

mutiti (Shona) *Erythrina abyssinica*; lucky bean tree. Thorny-branched, thick-corky-barked deciduous tree, widespread in wooded grassland and woodland

265

mutsatsati (Shona) *Faurea speciosa*; large-leafed beechwood tree. Most common in woodland and wooded grassland in the highveld

muvonde (Shona) *Ficus capensis*; Cape fig tree. Evergreen which reaches up to fifteen metres in height when full-grown. Occurs in woodland and wooded grassland

nkwazi (Shona) Fish-eagle